For Karen

all best!

thirteen fourteen fifteen o'clock

by
David Gerrold

This is a work of fiction.
Any similarity to persons living or dead
is entirely intentional.

Cover illustration and design by David Gerrold and Glenn Hauman
Interior design by ComicMix Pro Services
http://www.comicmix.com/pro-services

ISBN 978-1-939888-17-4 softcover

For information address
David Gerrold at his official website:
www.gerrold.com

for Dennis,
with love

thirteen o'clock

thirteen o'clock on a thirsty night, dry and windy after midnight, all the boys have paired up, disappeared into the desert, coupling darkly on the sand, have another beer, there's no place else to go except ride the hog and the hot air roars into your eyes at 70 miles per hour, getting too old for this shit, fucking boring, bored with fucking, bored with chasing fucking, bored with waking up alone, and even more bored waking up with anyone else, and even beer cant cure that, fuck me

except that's the problem, nobody wants to fuck me anymore, too many years, too many beers, and that other thing, the scar that starts above my right eye and crawls down to the corner of my mouth, pulling it down into a permanent scowl, so my face looks like something from a slasher movie, only the scar didnt happen when I was on the bike, but when I got off it, at high speed, using the right side of my head as a brake shoe, which wasnt as much fun as it sounds, not even with three beers

so I gave up on the queerbar for the night, the thing about queerbars, straightmen think you just walk in and get a blow job, everyboy is so fucking thirsty for cock, all you have to do is unzip your dockers, and if it were that easy, I wouldnt be standing in the bar at thirteen o'clock wondering what the hell I'm doing and how I got here and why I dont have any other place to go. So fuckit and before I'm halfway out the door, some guy is asking, hey, isnt that a queerbar, and before I can even turn and look, somebody's swinging something at my head and the old reflexes kick in and I duck sideways and he misses, but then the other guy's got a bike chain, stupid college kid, which I dont mean to grab, but I get it anyway because it skiddles off the cast on my arm before he can swing, indecision maybe, probably his first queer-bashing, blood-simple coward, then I'm holding the chain, one good yank, and he's holding a big handful of me, and his eyes go white just in time as I swing him around and shove him into his boyfriend with the baseball bat, and that's when I see the third one

someone oughta teach these little pricks how to beat up a fag, because they're no good at this at all, the third one crumples up too easily, a backhand across the windpipe, big ugly rings with scratchy things, and he's down, and then I'm back with chainless and bat, shoving chainless into bat and both up against the wall, so bat cant move and chainless is already screaming for mommy, godforbid someone should scar his pretty face like mine

—and something happens—

and that's when I get the idea that all he really needs is to be kissed so I pull him close and cover his scream with the bearded oyster and give him enough tongue to choke a deep throat, and I guess right because just as he's starting to kiss me back, surprising me more than him I think, and if this were a different time and a different place, I bet I could hang his legs over my shoulders, or mine over his, I'm not choosy, except the batboy is screaming and who can concentrate with all that noise

by the time danny-bartender finally makes it out the door with his own baseball bat, I've got two on the ground and one up against the wall with my hand on his throat, the pretty one, and I really do think

I could negotiate a relationship out of this, except that even as a "cute meet" this is a little too acute. So I let go of the cute meat, and he staggers forward, almost into my arms, jerks back, looks around, sees the queers piling out of the queerbar and maybe he thinks about running, but before he can send the message to his skechers, it's too late, he's caught

danny-bartender wants to call the police, but I tell him not to bother, because the one guy on the ground is having too much trouble breathing, I didnt think I hit him that hard, but he's got a nasty bubbling cut across his neck, which reminds me of things I saw in the service that I really dont want to think about at all, and the other guy who forgot about holding his bat when holding his stomach and his balls became a lot more important is having his own problems exsanguinating through his nose, so I go and pop open the back doors of my van and toss them in, I sold the hog six months ago and bought the van because it's easier on my bad leg and besides you can sleep in a van if you have to, and someboy asks where are you taking them and even though I want to take them out in the desert and bury them, without bothering to kill them first, I say the emergency room because I've already got enough death on my conscience

prettyboy rides in front with me, the other two moaning in the back, and nobody else wants to come because what queer wants to talk to cops anyway, I'm not worried, nobody fucks with me twice, not when I've got their wallets in my pocket

pull up at the E.R. and I drag them both out the back of the van and through the sliding doors, shouting, "white male, age 20, injury to his trachea, might need to intubate; white male, age 20, needs an X-ray for a cracked rib, broken nose, and someone call the police," and I only have to holler it twice before a doctor and two nurses come running tell the police I'm emmett grogan, they're too young to know the real emmett grogan, and besides I've got the i.d. that proves I'm emmett grogan, I made it myself, tell the police these two injured boys were just coming out of a gay bar, thirteen o'clock in the night, when they were attacked by queerbashers, lucky for them I was driving my little brother back to campus, I point to prettyboy, and we were just passing by

ex-marine, vietnam vet, ex-corpsman, got the tattoo in san diego, yessir, nossir, I didnt see the attackers clearly, officer, there were four of them, they looked like accountants, or maybe lawyers, probably republicans, you know they like to do that sort of thing, the cops give me the narrow-eyed look and I give them the deadpan, and then the fat one says, well if the victims were coming out of a queerbar they probbly got what they deserved, I dont see any need to pursue this further, and the skinny one adds, but maybe we should notify their parents, they look like college students, and I say, nah, give them a break, they're just kids, maybe this'll teach em to stay away from queerbars

and the fat cop says, nah, once they've been into a queerbar, you cant keep em out, one taste of cock and they're queer for life, so I just look at him deadpan and ask, is sucking cock that good, like he knows, and he blinks for a moment, realizing that he cant answer that question without looking either queer or stupid

back in the van, prettyboy still hasnt said a word, he's scared I'm gonna finish that kiss, or maybe he's hopin, but either way, he's sweating, so I hand him all three wallets, after taking out the cash, my own brand of justice, payment for lesson learned, nearly four hundred total, I drive him to his dorm, and as we pull up, he says, thank you for not reporting me to the cops, and at least he doesnt try to blame the other guys, it's all their fault, it wasnt his idea, he was just tagging along, which is obvious anyway, prettyboy is booksmart, but not much else, at least he knows enough not to say anything that stupid, so I think about all the bullshit I can say back to him and decide not to say any of it, instead I look him straight in the eye and say, the difference between us, someone calls me faggot, they're talking about what makes me happy, someone calls you faggot, they're talking about what makes you unhappy, you figure it out, all that money mommy and daddy are spending to send you away to university, you oughta be smart enough to figure out what you like

and then he does surprise me, he starts to open the door to get out and then he turns back and says, can we talk sometime, and there it is, half past whenever, dry and windy after midnight, and he's got big eyes and chewable lips, and surprise, surprise, my dick can still get hard, so I say yes and how about tomorrow night, and he says pick me up right here, and I'm already thinking, we'll go somewhere out on the other side of the desert where the truth is a lot easier, I know he'll never show up, not after twelve hours of sunlight-thinking, but what the fuck, nobody's waiting for me in the next town either, so why not

sleep away most of the day, crawl out of my coffin just in time to enjoy the sunset, shower and burger at the truck stop, think about beer, but leave it at thinking, not drinking, cruise over to the landing zone and prettyboy is leaning against a wall, he flicks his cigarette sideways, like he thinks that's butch, it isnt, and he strolls over and climbs in the passenger seat and I roll without talking and he doesnt say anything either and I'm wondering what the fuck he thinks is going to happen tonight, because I sure as shit dont have a clue, but this is something better than nothing we drive for a while, prettyboy finally says something, I was afraid you werent going to come, I tell him I didnt think he'd be there either, so we're even, he asks where we're heading, I shrug and nod ahead; away from the light, because I dont like the light, if it's too bright I can see the scars on my face from the inside, he tells me to stop calling him prettyboy, his name is Michael, I tell him he hasnt earned a name yet, he's still meat, fresh off the plane, and we've got a body bag already waiting with his name on it, deal with it

finally I ask him what the fuck he wants from me, he says he wants to know what I know and I tell him I dont know shit and finally we turn off the highway onto a side road and after a while off the side road onto a couple of forgotten ruts and we go two or three miles up and down bouncing to a place where something used to be, but now there's only hard-packed dirt, and I pull off and turn the engine off and we sit and listen to it cooling in the night

we get out, I go around to the back, pull out a blanket, a couple bottles of water, we sit in the dark, side by side, watching for shooting stars, and except for pointing them out to each other, we dont talk, I'm waiting for him to start, but he doesnt, so after a while, I reach over and grab his hand, not because I particularly want to hold his hand, I dont even fucking know him, but it's a start

he's not good for small talk, neither am I, he asks me how I know how to fight, I tell him the truth, fighting is easier than having the shit kicked out of you, then he asks me about my leg, so I tell him

somewhere in the fucking delta, the hot wind putrid, the whole country stinking like a Saigon whorehouse, disintegrating with the smell of shit and incense and rotting vegetation, all mixed with the spices they use to hide the fact that the meat is rotten before they even get it into the pan, even if you knew what it was—dog or cat or rat—who the fuck cares, when you get hungry enough, you stop asking questions

they call it a road, but it's just a lousy stinking dirt scar, a slash of mud carved between two fields, the crapgrass rippling in the wind—the distant edges bordered by trees, a fucking perfect place to die, a fucking bullseye for an ambush—the lieutenant holds up a hand and we all stop, then he holds his arm straight out and waves us down—we fade into the grass and disappear

they say that charlie is terrified of us, because we're monsters, bigger and healthier and better fed, better weapons, better ammo, better supplies—and better targets too—those little human cockroaches scuttle down into the ground and disappear, trapdoors in the floor of the world—everybody knows they're all underground, the delta is tunneled from here to forever, underground cities, you could walk all the way to uncle ho without ever seeing daylight—and maybe they're right, maybe the little fuckers are scared shitless, but I dont think so

claymore—we call him that because he's good at taking mines apart—he grins and whispers across to me, it's a good day to die. I tell him to shut the fuck up. it's never a good day to die, but he saw that in a movie and he thinks it's cool—it isnt cool, it's fucking stupid—and what are we waiting for anyway?

the lieutenant is yabbering into the field phone, the sweat is rolling down the inside of my shirt, the sun is a hundred and thirty degrees and we're all carrying fifty pounds of field gear—whose good idea was this anyway?—the field isnt a field, it's a fucking swamp, we're up to here in mud so deep that every step, the mud is fighting to pull my boots off—and I cant stand too long in one place, I start to sink deeper

oh man, I am going to stand for an hour in the

shower tonight and I dont fucking care what color the water is

the lieutenant he stands up and waves us back to the road—whatever—he does this five, six times an hour—squelching up out of the mud, and before I can yank my boot free, the world fucking blows up in my face—all the different colors of orange and white and red and black, all at once, and everybody's screaming because the shit is going off all around us—they're dropping fucking mortar shells on us, and they've got our range because the crap is hitting left and right and up and down—claymore flies apart in pieces, a fucking good day to die my fucking ass—and I'm too busy pulling my goddamn leg out of the mud to be scared—we're all firing wildly at the distant trees, like we're really going to hit something, we're fucking dead out here

rocks and shit and mud comes pattering down, all around, a pummeling of earth, it goes on forever while the ground shakes and your ears bleed and the world turns sideways and knocks you assover everywhere, and no my leg isnt supposed to bend like that, but I cant feel it anyway, and I cant find my fucking gun and while my hand is flailing around everything turns orange, the sky, the muck, a wall of heat knocks me flat into the shit, rolls me sideways, and then I hear the first roar of the flames—a roiling carpet, napalm forest, blossoming scars across the whole west side of the world, and for a moment, there's a kind of peace, the explosions stop, shocked in fucking horror, roasted alive, who fucking cares, I fade out and over, something is whupping up and I feel nothing

while I'm dead everything is fine, because I cant feel anything, I dont care, I could go on like this forever, white light and voices

—something happened—

but then it's gone, leaving only a memory of

a memory, a sense that there was something *important*, maybe it was the drugs, but no, I know drugs and this wasnt drugs, this was something *else,* but it's gone, it's like hearing the echo, but not knowing what clanged, the feeling stays with me all the way across the pacific and down into the crevices of San Francisco, it never fades, a sense of muffled awareness, the doctors tell me it's resonance, it'll go away, but they're wrong, it doesnt—never completely, it just drifts behind-inside forever, it doesn't bother me, it just turns into something to live with, like the plastic leg

so I spend a few years riding a hog up and down the left coast, cruising up through Big Sur, across the big red bridge, up through Marin, into the cold wet wild north where the trees make green canyons, up into Oregon where the green is too thick and I start thinking about Charlie creeping through the green, if Charlie had green like this, we'd still be there, it's nothing like the Delta, first of all the smell is sweet and green and wet, but I cant shake the feeling that something is creeping up after me, so I keep riding, on up as far as Puget where the only difference between the fog and the rain is that the fog is thicker and wetter and from there up to the border where the Canadian customs guard is so exquisitely polite I know he hates to let me in, but he cant find a reason not to, I'm legal, I just look ugly, so on into Canada, eh, all the way up to Alaska and I lose myself for a few years with the bears and the salmon and the air so crisp it cuts like ice through the tent, through the sleeping bag, and man I'm getting too old for this shit, but I gotta know what it was, and for some reason I've made up my mind that the Inuit know, some shaman or medicine man, whatever, because maybe underneath, there's some magic here

and maybe there is, but I never find it, so I come sliding back south, dropping down through Idaho, following the Snake river all the way down, passing through forgotten dusty places with names too small for the map, endless dry highways, into Nevada with its desolate empty stretches of baking summer

east to Utah where the canyons still echo with fossilized time, south to New Mexico with its hidden villages carved into orange sunset cliffs, west to Arizona and up the poisonous side of Superstitious Mountain, maybe there's a wise old grandfather, the Hopi know life out of balance, and eventually south through Mexico, where I spend a week or a year or whatever living the way of the whaqui, eating mushrooms and peyote and rattlesnakes, fucking everything that I can push down on its back or its stomach, if it's a hole and I'm horny, I dont care anymore, it doesnt matter, there's that instant of orgasm, that quick throb-and-spurt of time where I stop existing long enough that the nagging sense of something unsaid and left undone is pushed so far out of my consciousness that it almost doesnt exist for that moment, and the lassitude afterward, on my back and staring dispassionately at the glowering sky, waiting for wisdom and insight, that connection of time and place and understanding, but all I accomplish is a thousand light-year stare with nothing on the other side, and one day I put the hog back together, get the engine running, tune it, tweak it, test it, over and over, until it sounds like magic growling again, until one day it's right, and the moment is right, and I get on and start riding, just a test ride, I say, but I keep riding north and never look back, I run out of luck at a queer hippie commune south of Tucson and live in a teepee while I flush out all the crap from my system, lose twenty pounds of Mexican bad shit and end up with abs again, stumping up and down the rows of corn and beans and tomatoes, digging latrines, carrying water, hoeing and weeding, learning to serve others again, and for the first time in longer than I can remember actually earning the right to feel good about myself at the end of the day

but its all queerboys here and there's stuff going on that I dont want to deal with—and after I drive away, I realize, I'm not ready to give up girlpussy forever, it's fixed in my mind now that there's boypussy and girlpussy, and each is fine in its own way, and by now I've even learned there's other things to do and maybe that's part of the answer, if not *the* answer, it's still part of it, because what these queerboys have learned is that it's not about fucking, it's about people, a strange place to learn this

and then, in an angry flash, I dont know how it happens, I'm back on the left again, Arizona a red and gold memory in the rear-view mirror, how did that happen?—the moving finger writes and once it writes you're fingered, I come bouncing down into the Castro where I hook up with Bloody Mary, a bulldyke who rides a hog and sometimes she rides me and sometimes she rides the hog and once she rides us both at the same time and I ask her how can she be a dyke if she's riding the rod and she just laughs and says it isnt about pussy, it's about people, so I'm not the only one who's figured that out

we coast up to Guerneville where nobody cares, where we're out of earshot of the creepazoids who think we're traitors to the fag-flag because we're bumping each other ugly, except one night I break my leg in Sausalito, laying down the bike to avoid a drunken spoiled teenage bitch, and if I could have gotten up afterward I'd have punched her a new one, but I cant get up because the bike is on top of me, she jumps out and starts wailing about the dent I just put in the side of her new car that daddy just bought her only two days ago for her seventeenth birthday, while I'm still lying under a bleeding hog and

—it happens again—

until Mary the dyke slaps her, takes away her new expensive toy, this thing called a cell phone, and punches 911 and calls an ambulance, and I'm off to the E.R. tonight and the V.A. tomorrow, and fortunately it's the plastic leg that's broken and six weeks later, the V.A. finally puts me on a new one, a better one, and I'm ready to get back in the saddle, except

I dont want to, something's happened; I cant explain it, but something's happened, and even though I feel like a cowboy who has to shoot his horse, I sell the hog, what's left of it, and no, it isnt fear, I could get back on the bike in half a minute, I trust myself on the road, I dont trust anyone else, I trust my ability to keep out of their way, but if a seventeen-year-old bitch can put me down in the gutter, maybe it's the universe sending me a message; the dyke tells me I'm a pussy, so I know she doesnt understand, and fuckit, I'm not even sure I understand it myself, all I know is it's time to let go, the bike isnt me anymore, and neither is the dyke

and then time flashes and I'm living out of the back of a VW bus, I dont even remember where I got it, but the feeling is there, I can drive out to the middle of the Mojave, get off the highway, get off the side road, find a dirt slash into the middle of nowhere, someplace even the lights in the distance are too far away to look like anything more than stars glimmering through the bottom of the world, and I lay down on my back and look up at the diamond sky and it's like riding the hog again, only this time riding it through time and space, I'm standing at the front of starship earth and sailing forward like I'm king of the universe and I can hear the feeling loud and clear like picking up clear channel KOMA from five states away

and I know it's not the tequila and it's not the grass and it's not a fucking acid flashback either, it's something else, and I can feel the throb and pulse of the ground beneath my body and I know the ground doesnt throb and pulse, so what the flaming fuck am I feeling, it's just my own heartbeef, slabs of muscle too stubborn to stop slamming the blood through my veins, and what the fuck is life all about anyway, but the feeling, it wont go away, it's like music sometimes, a distant chorus, very faint and far away, under the edge of the horizon, like those things whatever they are that always woke me when I was little, going *hoo-hooo* in the night

and I tell prettyboy, that's what I know, that I'm just another hood ornament on the battering ram, wherever it goes, I get there first, hardest—I'm the part that takes the impact—but every time, just before the collision, I get this flash, like there's something under the bottom of the world, calling to me, I dont know what the fuck it is, but I cant get away from it, cant get it to shut up, cant forget it, and cant fucking die until I find out what it is

so now it's his turn to explain and he tells me there's nothing to explain, he isnt anybody at all, he doesnt, just doesnt, and it doesnt matter that there's no predicate to that subject, I get it because I've been there, I'm still there, I live there, we all do, only some of us know it

he says it started in bed, in bed with a girl, she was warm and round and luscious like something out of a painting by Rubens or maybe Titian and he just wanted to float on top of her like she was a giant delicious waterbed, he wanted to suckle at her breasts and bury his face in her juicy cunt and it surprised him when I said, yeah, I know, except whatever else she was, she wasnt either, and she wouldnt

they'd lie together, spooned, his arm curled around her side, but once when his fingers start tentatively brushing at her thigh, she mumbles not now, and another time when he brushes at her lips, the lower ones, probing for her clit, she pushes his hand away roughly as if he's an intruder, and still another time when he moves his fingers up to circle her great pancake-sized nipples, she rolls away, is that all you ever think about, so he turns on his side and tries to sleep while this great moby of desirability rests naked behind him, his cock still stiff, his balls aching, and the next morning as he's pulling his tighty-whites up and over the tentpole, she sits up in bed and complains that he's unromantic, that he doesnt want to do it with her, and it's because she's fat, isnt it, and to his credit he doesnt say anything, he just finishes pulling up his pants, he buttons his shirt and slips into his sneakers and closes the door behind him, all without a word or even a look, because inside he's feeling so—there isnt really a word for that feeling, but that's what he's feeling, so he leaves and three nights later he's outside a queerbar with two guys he barely knows, it doesnt make sense, but nothing in life makes sense, why would anyone want to fuck a guy when there are all these beautiful fat women around, except if they dont want to fuck, what's a guy to do, get desperate, and he's almost ready to cry, except he's still too full of that other feeling

so there we are, I have too much life and he doesnt have any, so I hold his hand and after a while he leans up against me, and we sit there listening, he listens for what I can hear and I listen for silence

are you going to fuck me, he asks, and I dont answer for a while because I dont know the answer, I dont know if I want to fuck him, he's pretty enough and after that kiss, I didnt figure it would be that hard to get his ankles behind his neck, or mine, it doesnt matter, but I dont know if it's worth the effort, fucking for the sake of fucking sounds fine when you're fifteen, but not when the digits are reversed, so I'm sitting there wondering why he asked, is it something he wants or is it something he's afraid I'm going to do to him whether he wants it or not, and just the fact he asked the question scares the shit out of me, not the scared-shitless feeling like when live fire is making a three-foot ceiling over your head, but the other-scared feeling of just not knowing who you are or what you're supposed to do, a feeling I thought I'd left behind in Alaska or Mexico, or maybe certainly in Arizona, or probably somewhere since then, but finally I just say, is that what you want and he doesnt answer, because I figure he's probably sorting it out the same way

then the moment passes, and I know we're not going to fuck, not then, and probably not ever, but I've been wrong about that before, so we both just relax, now that the question's been asked, not answered, but resolved anyway for the moment, and I'm sitting there thinking a whole fucking epic, and he says, thank you, and I ask, for what, and he says, for listening

and yeah, I get it, and I say so, and he asks, does this feeling ever go away, and even though I'm not sure what feeling he's talking about I still know the answer, I shake my head, I say no, it never does, you just learn to live with it; he breaks away, he sits opposite so he can look at me, the moon is up now, half-past full, so there's enough light I can see his eyes are bright, and yeah, he's getting prettier by the moment, and I'm almost rethinking the answer to his question, but I'm not, because it still isnt happening and in the moonlight, I know why

there's this guy I knew once, his name was Jerry, we went to the same high school, we never talked to each other, we just saw each other in the hallway sometimes, and sometimes at the Big Boy where he was bussing tables, working his way through community college, but we werent in any of the same classes there either, we just saw each other around, and then I forgot about him, the way you forget most of the people you bump up against as you stumble along, until one night a few years later, it's the collapsing end of 1969, and I'm in a boy-bar on Santa Monica Boulevard, and I see him sitting alone in the corner in the back patio and he looks like Wiley Coyote right after the rocket exploded in his face, so I go over and say hi, and he says hi back and I ask him what's wrong, and he cant even get it out, he just looks at me with a look I've only seen one other time, a year later, in the Delta, when Perry the black kid with the big round eyes caught one and just looks at me, his hands across his belly, all his dark red blood pulsing out between his fingers, trying to push his guts back in, and he looks at me, our eyes meet for just a second, and the expression on his face says it all, please tell me I'm going to be all right, tell me I'm not going to die, and he knows I wont lie to him, and I lie and say, hey man, just hold on, just hold on, and the medic stings him with morphine and his eyes stay fixed on mine the whole time, and then the blood stops pulsing and he's dead, but his eyes are still wide, and that's the look that I saw on Jerry's face, like he was asking me to tell him that he wasnt dead yet

but that hadnt happened yet, this was the first time I ever saw this look, and it stopped me cold, because I didnt know a human face could look like that, and it froze me—the terror, the desperate need, I thought I should do something, except I wasnt in that bar to be Mary Poppins, I was looking for some boypussy, and I was this close to saying, fuckit, tell it to the chaplain, tell it to someone who cares, someone who's paid to care—but then he says, tell me why I shouldnt kill myself and I didnt have the sense to back away quickly, so I stand over him, instinctively shielding him from the light and the noise and the stink of cigarettes and beer and Old Spice and I listen—and what he tells me, well, it almost saves my life

see, he wasnt making it, it was the end of the fucking sixties for god sake, everything was falling apart in slow motion, and all anybody could do was get stoned and fuck their brains out, so that's what we did, all night long, every night, there wasnt any daytime anymore, just the long long night of parties—only Jerry was alone, one of those guys who never quite finds the rhythm of anything, he didnt know how to be whatever it was he was supposed to be, nobody did, and everybody's walking around saying stupid shit like, "hey man, where's it happening?" and you have no fucking idea how dumb that sounds, it's like admitting you're so lost you cant even see the party even when it's happening around you, it was happening everywhere and it wasnt happening anywhere, because whatever was happening, it was only happening when you made it happen, but most of us never learned that lesson, or died trying, so even though Jerry didnt understand it, that was the thing that made him just like everybody else because nobody understood it yet, but Jerry was one of the smart ones, so smart he was stupid; he thought the world was gettable, and because he thought that, he thought that there were people who actually did get it, in fact Jerry thought that everybody did, probably already had, except they'd all privately agreed not to let him in on it, none of it made sense and nobody was letting him in on the joke, so after a while he gives up, just gives up completely and resigns, stops waiting for Santa Claus and starts waiting for rigor mortis, he's ready to be just another one of those used-up boys propped up against the bar like scenery—the ones who've been entered too many times and finally abandoned all hope, the ones who settle for fucking as a substitute for loving, nowhere near a fair trade, but if you fuck long enough and hard enough, sometimes you dont notice, trust me on this

except fucking-God's a practical joker, because just when Jerry decides there aintno such thing as either God or love, that's the afternoon, God drops a beautiful redheaded boy on him, and the two of them do something right and instead of just falling lustfully into bed, mindlessly fucking their brains out on each other's flesh until half-past seeyaround, instead it's too hot to fuck, so they sit and talk for five hours on this sweaty July afternoon, and instead of thinking only about their dicks, they actually work a little higher up, the other end of the spinal cord, and not until the day finally cools off do they end up in bed, but that's only because it's a more comfortable place to just strip down to your jockeys and relax, surrender to the moment, because it doesn't matter anymore, you dont have to pretend now, just be who you are, and they still dont fuck, they share a big glass of ice water and keep talking, and it doesnt matter what they're talking about, they're just having this amazing adventure talking and discovering, and even after they get naked—and you know how you get naked in front of other guys, there's this thing, you know the thing, where you really dont want them looking at you, because you know they're sizing you up, judging how good you look or how big you are, and you know you're never going to look as good as the guys in the magazines, and you end up feeling that you dont want to be naked in front of anyone because you dont want them thinking you're not good enough—except that doesnt happen here, they end up sitting together naked, unashamed, each one astonished at how beautiful the other one is, and they still dont fuck, they hug and kiss and touch in wonder, and they laugh a lot at some shared joke of intimacy, and finally take a shower together and laugh a whole lot more, and then they hump and bump a little, even a lot, but they keep interrupting themselves to talk and to share, and before either one of them has come anywhere near to that moment where it's time to get a towel and wipe off and make a hasty graceless exit, they realize that—*something is happening*—it's silly, so fucking silly, because there's no such thing as love at first sight, it's just a fairy tale, but there they are anyway, falling ass-over-teakettle, tumbling over the cliff of joyous delirium, so full of happy giggling exuberance it doesnt make sense, until Jerry has impossible tears running down his cheeks and he wants to run out in the middle of the street and yell to the whole world, dont you dumbfucks get it, love—*real love*—really is possible, and if Hitler had ever had sex this good, World War II would never have happened, that's what it feels like, fucking so good you feel sorry for Hitler, and he and the redheaded boy roll together, laughing

but look, it isnt about the sex at all, it was never about the sex, everybody thinks it's about the cocks and the cunts and the mouths and the assholes, all that juicy pistoning, the hot wet pumping in-and-out, but it isnt, it's about the thing that happens *during* sex, if it's right, if everything is right between the two people, whoever, whatever, if there's a real connection, then the sex is just a way to get even more connected, because it's the connection you want, not the sex—because the truth is, when you're fucking, it's not about you, it's about the person you're with, because if it isnt, then you're the biggest dumbfuck of all, just licking the menu instead of eating the meal—and that's the magic that Jerry and his beautiful redheaded boy fell into

yeah, I know, it doesnt make sense to sit and talk with someone from four o'clock in the afternoon until nine in the fucking ayem the next morning, when you have to get up and go back to work, and on the basis of that short time know that this is the person you want to spend the rest of your life with, that all you want from existence is to keep on exploring the landscape of this beautiful incredible godling, discovering yourself in his smile and his laughter and his cockness, but it happened to them, both of them, they connected anyway, and in the days after that first incredible revelation of each other, it just gets better, they start learning how to do all the other things that people do when they fit their lives together—they talk to each other on the phone every day for three weeks, grabbing every moment they can between their respective jobs and obligations and it should have been perfect, because each of them was exactly what the other one wanted and needed, they fit, you know, they just fit, and every moment was well, you know, just perfect

and then it all comes apart, because Jerry makes a stupid mistake, the biggest stupidest mistake anyone can make, he gets scared, he stops trusting his instincts, because see, the redheaded boy wants to get serious, I mean serious with a capital lets-move-in-together, and Jerry panics, because he thinks it's getting too intense, he cant deal with it, he doesnt know how—I mean, how do you explain it to mom, right?—because nobody gives lessons to queerboys how to have a real relationship, and make it work in a world that mindlessly believes that this thing that brings you so much joy is so despicable that God hates you for it, and the whole thing scares him, so instead of being home, he leaves a note on the door and goes out cruising instead, not because he wants to cruise, but because he doesnt know what else to do, but he's so fucking confused, so the redheaded boy takes the note off the door and goes out looking for something else to do and he picks up a hitchhiker, no, not quite, that's not where this story is going, let me finish, and the hitchhiker is caretaker at some estate up in Benedict Canyon, so the redheaded boy drives him up there and they talk for a while, but they dont really connect, so after a while, the redheaded boy picks up the phone and calls Jerry, and Jerry is back home by now—see, here's what happened, Jerry cruises and cruises and realizes that cruising is empty, because now that he knows that there's something else, cruising is meaningless, and now that he knows what the something else is, he knows what a jerk he's been for leaving that note, for not being home, and all he really wants to do tonight is curl up with his beautiful redheaded lover and not have to talk, just be in his arms and never be apart again, he's ready to jump off the diving board and say yes, I will

only on the way down the hill, the redheaded boy runs into some drug-crazed hippies, and they shoot him in the face, and then they go into the house and murder four other people, five if you count the unborn baby, and Jerry stays up all night wondering where his lover is, and he doesnt find out what happened until he opens the newspaper Sunday morning, still with me, and he goes crazy, and I dont mean crazy like banging into the walls, raging with grief, I mean crazy like you dont know, nobody knows, because they dont know how to show it in the movies yet, I mean crazy like staring into space crazy, zombie-crazy, desperate crazy, and who the fuck can he talk to about it, because who in the world would understand, certainly no straight man, maybe another faggot, except all he knows about boy-bar faggots is that he doesn't trust any of them either, he knows who they are because he's one of them too

and it's two-three months later, and the murderers still havent been caught, and he tells me all of this in the back patio of a sleazy boy-bar in West Hollywood because he has no other place to go, and of all the places to go, this is the worst, because it just puts him back where he was before, but he cant be what he was before, because this time, now, he knows what he doesnt have, and that's when the tears start running down his cheeks, all he had was three weeks, hardly enough time to make any memories at all, just a couple of fucks and a drive around the city, and all he can think of is that he's never going to see his lover again, the most precious person in his life, never again, and all the memories they're never going to have, all the pillow conversations, and why the hell should he keep on living if the best part of his life is over

but see, here's how I know that God is a malignant thug, a practical joker, an asshole—if he wouldnt listen to his own son's prayers on the cross, why the fuck do you think he's going to listen to anyone else's?—here's the joke, Jerry looks at me like I'm supposed to say the one thing, whatever it is, that makes a difference, except I dont know what the fuck it is, how the hell should I know how to save his life, because I cant even save my own, because I've got my goddamned draft notice in my back pocket and I have to report the day after Thanksgiving, and in three-four months, just in time for the rains, I'll be slogging through the goddamn Delta with all the other dead men walking, and I'm thinking what the fuck, maybe I should run for Canada instead, I can be there in a straight two day run, or maybe I should just tell them I like sucking cock and fucking ass, at least that's honest, except I'm not ready to be that honest yet, nobody is, except I also heard that they dont even care anymore, the draft boards, they just have to generate so many bodies a week, fill up the green uniforms, fill up the body bags, and this week it's me and next week it's you, it's all the same, and Jerry looks up at me and says, so okay, now you tell me—why shouldnt I kill myself?

I dunno, why shouldnt he? He's made a pretty

damn good case, except forever is a long time, and I'm thinking if I were a sky-pilot, I'd know the right thing to say, except I'm not, and I dont, and besides, if I said the crap they say, we'd both know it's crap, so I say what's in my head, and I say, I am so fucking jealous of you I can't believe it, and his eyes go wide, and I just keep talking anyway, because man, you found it, even if it was only for three weeks, you had it, man—I never did, and you know something most of the rest of us can only wish for, and he looks at me, not getting it, and I dont know where the words are coming from, I just blurt it out—real love, man, you had it, someone really loved you, the rest of us we're standing around and pretending that we're not standing around and pretending, but you—man, you're lucky everybody else in here doesnt beat you to death out of sheer fucking jealousy, because what you had, you had the *real*, not the pretend, You. Had. *It.*

and maybe that was what he needed to hear, and maybe what he said was what I needed to hear—that it really was possible, because up until then, I didnt know it, maybe nobody did, Jerry was the first person I ever knew who found love, the first one who could actually say it, and while he's crying for what he's lost, I'm wishing I were him, I want what he had, even if it's only for three weeks or three days or three hours

and as I'm telling all this, as it's all pouring out of me in one dumb rush, I look across at the prettyboy and see only blankness in the eyes and I realize he doesnt know what I'm talking about, cant know, because he's never done it, never been there, never had that rush of endorphins, that wave of physical amazement that starts in the bottom of your dick and comes tidal-waving up your spine like some kind of astonishing hot tsunami and floods up inside of you, inside your heart, your whole chest, chokes up your throat, and floods your eyes with tears of wonder and joy, he's never known it, that's the fucking tragedy, he's never been there

and the question of sex with him, of fucking him, it's finally answered for me, because if there's no connection, then all it is, it's just fucking exercise, and I've had enough exercise for ten lifetimes—I dont want to wake up with an intimate stranger, someone who knows the taste of my sweat, but not the taste of me, just another zombie-fuck

but there was that moment, I know it happened, when he *kissed back* and something flickered in that moment and that's the moment I'm speaking to—who was that?—and how do I get back there, how does anyone

did he kill himself, prettyboy asks, it's the wrong question, I shake my head and mutter something, I dont know, I never saw him again, maybe he did, maybe he didnt, maybe he just stumbled out into the night, like everybody else, you crawl into your coffin and dont come out again until it's time to feed, but I do know, I just dont want to say it

I stand, stretch, listen to the bones tap-dancing against each other, stretch again, denying entropy one more time, start picking up blankets and water bottles, is that it, he asks, and I turn and look at him, what did you want, and he doesnt answer, doesnt have an answer, and maybe that's the greater tragedy, worse than knowing what you want and never having it is never knowing, never being able to speak it at all

headed back in silence, bumping over the hard-packed dirt, finally up and onto the asphalt again, sliding through the dark, the wind roaring like a jet engine, and still he doesnt talk, for some reason he doesnt look so pretty anymore, and I'm wondering why I bothered, why I wasted my time, and why I didnt fuck him anyway, except even an old boar like me has some pride

—something happened—

I never talk about the *blinks*, nobody understands, I tried a couple times, but I got the look, that look, the one that says I'm going to pretend I understand you, but only for as long as it takes to gnaw off my leg and escape, and no we cant ever be drinking buddies again because you're crazier than me, there's something scary-wrong in your head, so I learned the hard way, I just dont talk about the *blinks*, not to anyone, and when they happen, they happen, nobody around me notices, so maybe I am crazy, it's like somebody cutting into the movie, just a dazzling flash of bright, way too fast to see, you only realize it afterward, except afterward there's the burn-in still hanging in the air, the after-images of whatever seared into my existential retinas

never found anybody who knew about it, even with careful asking, none of the gurus, nor the medicine men, the shamans, not the dopers and dealers neither, asked a few doctors and corpsmen if they'd ever heard of anything like it, but they just looked at me funny, so I dropt the subject

only once, the crazy dyke, late one night on the road, somewhere between nowhere and nothing, we finally pull over and fall out onto our blankets, eventually end up on our backs, first her, then me, then both of us, staring up at the stars—*something happens*—and I ask her, did you feel that, and she asks, feel what, and I try to explain, and she says, you got *pinged*, and I say, pinged, what's that, and she says, it's when somebody is checking you out, seeing if you're there, like submarines in the dark, I ask, no she says, it's like computers on a network, I *ping* you and you *pong* back, except you aint ponging, but someone's definitely pinging

and that's as far as that conversation goes, but it sticks, enough so that whenever—*something happens*—I'm listening to hear who it is, or *what*, aliens or angels or Ida Noh, the mystery whore of Saigon, how'd you get the clap, soldier, Ida Noh, sir—I'm listening, listening like the antenna at Arecibo

except I'm always listening *after*, never during, never before, it's like lightning, you only know you've been struck by it when you pick yourself up off the ground afterward, like Jerry and his redhead, and I figure that maybe I'm the wrong kind of receiver, or maybe I'm not getting the whole signal, or maybe I'm in the fringe area, Ida Noh again, and the only part of any of it that I can be sure of is that it never happens when I'm alone, it only happens when I'm with someone and only when the moment is intense, very intense, too intense, almost overload, that's when it happens, when the meter is pinned

other people, they talk about those moments when everything happens at once, when the car starts to skid, when it goes skidding/swerving/screeching/sideways, that's the moment when time stops for them, for me that's the moment when time disappears, and I come out the other side still ringing all over, reconnecting to myself, I know I'm missing something here, I used to think that if I could find someone else, anyone who experienced the same thing, then maybe we could, Ida Noh, connect, and if it happened to us together, at the same time, maybe we could get a clearer signal, except when I talk about the blinks, the pings, I get the stare, the what-are-you-talking-about look, so that's not an option

except yeah, at the back of my mind, I'm still always thinking, maybe this one, maybe this time, maybe finally I'll find out who's calling, who's pinging, and sometimes I'll go days/weeks/months without a ping and I'll miss it for a while and then I'll get used to the silence and then I'll even forget about the pings for a while, until it starts again, and once, lying awake in some strange bed in the middle of some strange night, I had this thought that maybe I'm only one piece of the circuit, like a transistor or a capacitor or one of those other bits of electric magic, and maybe what I need isnt another piece like me, but some other piece totally unlike me, maybe I'm just an antenna, maybe I need a modulator or a resonator or maybe just a tuning knob, maybe there's a whole bunch of pieces missing, and maybe I'm not anything at all, just a chimpanzee hammering on a rock and striking the occasional spark

that's the other thought, that whatever it is, maybe it's something I cant know, maybe none of us can, because we're not there yet, we can string some wires and make electricity run around in circles and sparkle some lights, but we still cant do that next thing, whatever it is, that next thing that comes after super-sharp televisions and super-fast computers, that thing that we still havent thought of, whatever it will be, and by comparison with that, we're still just apes with bones and flints, and that's the thing I think about listening to the stars, listening for others, maybe we're listening with the wrong ears, and we cant really hear whoever is pinging, maybe only a few of us can hear occasional bits and pieces of the pings and the rest of us cant hear anything at all because we're just not there yet, we're still in bed with Ida Noh in the hot damp nights of Saigon

and oh shit, Saigon, and Perry, late one night, we play cut-for-low and loser takes the point next day on patrol, and it's Perry who catches it in the belly, not me, and it's Jerry all over again, only this time it's me with the guilt, with the story, it's my fault he died, I only lose a leg, but Perry spills his guts, and ever since then I've been spilling mine, only I never get to die, Perry was the lucky one, he got out quick

and I get it, I get it *again*, we're all dragging dead bodies around, offering each other a sniff of the corpse, the past is this heavy ruck that sits on our backs, growing heavier every year, we just keep adding more and more shit to the load, and eventually history is inescapable, the shitbird guru on my shoulder yabbers into my ear, the past defines not just the present, but the future as well, there's no escape, is there, this is it, and that's why I didnt fuck the prettyboy, because there's no place in my past for that future

finally bring him back to where we started, the big empty parking lot below the dorm, pull to a stop, we look at each other, all the stuff still unsaid, the real stuff that nobody ever says, and just before the seeya—*something happens*—and the van starts shaking, hard, like something slamming against it from the side, again and again, and then the lights of the world come on, dazzling, finger-stabbing, searching, finally pinning us in the van, and there's a great whooshing noise and screaming too, all the voices in the world, prettyboy grabs my hand and

—*it happens*—

He's turned pretty again. Pretty frightened. Everything slows down, stops. The eye of the timestorm. Even while the banging continues around us.

—*connection*—

all the flickers, all the blinks, everything, time and space collapses into one moment, and this time I'm in the moment, caught, a dragonfly in amber, gossamer wings transparent in the heavenly backlight, and in the same instant, everything simultaneous

—*I get it*—

There's Jerry and Perry and Mary the bulldyke and even prettyboy, and all the rest of us, everyone who connected, who flickered in and out, all of us woven like ganglia into the great neural web of sentience recognizing itself. That's who's been pinging—not aliens or angels or anything else—*it's us.* All of us together. That's the connection. Our own humanity is calling. It's the next step. It isnt a secret, it never was, except all of us together, we never knew, or we keep forgetting, or we do it on purpose, but now this time—*some of us* can actually see it happening—

—*the fireflower blossoms*—

A hot rush, a tidal wave, tsunami of exuberance, rising up through me, I can see to the end of the universe and back, all of us, connecting, lighting up, answering the pings, awakening to ourselves, blinking alive, confused, excited, wondrous, not everyone yet, but all of us who've heard the wake-up call, and in that moment, we're together, and we *know*, and it's *now*, and there's *no* going back

—*Oh*—

and then as the van topples and crashes sideways onto the street, the sirens come whooping in, the red and blue lights flickering, flashing turning—the moment is broken, and I'm scrambling up over prettyboy to unlatch his door, push it open, start to climb out, when the first bottle comes crashing against it, and a baseball bat *whangs* into the windshield, fracturing it, but not shattering, so that isnt the way, I fumble sideways, crawling, kick the back doors open with my good leg and come out with the aluminum bat in one hand, ready to bang the hell out of last night's bashers, who've been waiting for me all night long with their fraternity brothers and a keg of beer, the whole gang of chimpanzees, believing that I've kidnapped one of their own, they're going to rescue him from the bearded monster

except the cops are already here, beanbag rifles at the ready, lights flashing, spotlights dazzling me, the chopper above pins me in a funnel of light, so I drop the bat and raise my hands and lie down slowly on the asphalt, because already I know how this will play out

I clean up real good, no piercings, no tats, shave and a haircut, put on a clean suit, yes, I have one, but leave the prosthesis at home, fold up the pants leg, and limp into court on a crutch, tell the judge the bashers broke it when they pushed my van over, a seven-thousand dollar peg, one battered old vet with no leg to stand on, opposite a bunch of frats with attitude, there's no question what will happen here, six of them get expelled, the chapter gets its charter pulled, and the town has something to argue about until Christmas break, I'll be gone by then anyway, autumn rolls away and with it me, no more dry desert nights for this old bear, maybe I'll drift south to the tip of Baja and lie naked in the unforgiving sun like a great baking whale, or maybe north into Canada again, or Alaska, where I'll snuggle deep in a tiny cabin, hibernating like a grumpy old wolverine, listening to the snow piling up against the windows, anywhere away from here, away from the madness and the noise, the squalor of human ignorance, all the vicious scrabbling little souls that still dont get *it*, might never get it, will never get it because all the clamor they make drowns out all the other possibilities, they're screaming so loud about what they want they cant hear that the answer is already yes

when your watch says thirteen o'clock, what time is it—it's time to get a new watch, the pieces of this one are scattered all over the floor—it's time to build a new one

—something is happening, it's still happening—

All the parts of me/us, we're scattered, yes, but we're pinged and connected and we can sense/feel/hear each other. We're something new. A little two year-old girl, standing up in her crib, crying with a wet diaper, but that's not why she's crying, she's not yet ready for the burden of knowledge. A black grandmother, suddenly awake in the night, wondering why she's thinking of her dead grandson all of a sudden, he died in Nam, but she can hear him somewhere—with all time and space collapsed, he's right here now. A skinny teenage boy, secretly trying on his sister's panties, abruptly confused and wondering why he can suddenly see into the future, scared of what he's becoming and intrigued as well. The cop holding the beanbag rifle, blinking, scanning the whole situation through a dozen different pairs of eyes, instead of just his own little piece; he sees through the perp's eyes, feels the fear and terror. A young woman, screaming, channeling a joyous excruciating birth, the baby screams with her, mother and child locked together in mutual awareness. The desperate man, standing on the bridge, the choice in his eyes, suddenly alive beyond his own horizons, stepping back to reconsider. The student, looking up from his book—there's a world out there, a vast unknowable, incomprehensible world; the book, the words, the crawling insect marks upon the page, the barest shadow of meaning, there is no explanation, it's just what's happening.

Is still happening. Now.

And all the others too, touched with wonder—frightened, intrigued, cautious, but stepping into the moment, it'll take a while. We'll get there. This thing, whatever it is we are, all of us still sorting it out, we're a long way from threshold and even farther from critical mass, we're alone, but not alone, never alone, never again.

And Michael, I glance over at him, dazed and confused, but waking up into himself now. I wonder how many more are waking up.

fourteen o'clock

fourteen o'clock and the bar is still loud, the air foggy with sweat, shirtless dancers writhing in near dark, a brief pause, the lights turned up for last call, the bottles collected in haste, the dancing resumes, the music pounding like something trying to break through the gates of hell, I'm not sure which side we're on though, and whether the something is trying to break in or break out or just break on through for the fun of breaking

I dont dance, not with this leg, but I still like watching naked bodies twist and bounce, all in flickering red light, sparkling and booming, as frenzied as that day in Chu Lai—but this time no one dies, no one screams, no one bleeds, why am I here?—it's therapeutic, deliberately reprogramming my head with irreverence, overwhelming the past with the present, one day I'll get it right, and even if I dont, at least there's a chance of getting laid

a figure blocks my view, a black silhouette blocking the splashes of color, the sparkles of light, I lean to the left, he steps that way to block my view—annoyed, I lean the other way, he steps the other way too, I'm in his shadow

then my eyes focus, a moment of what-the-fuck, and I recognize him

he leans in, shouts in my good ear, I thought I'd find you here he's gone all scruffy, not the clean little pretty boy anymore, hair down to here, black eye-shadow, a sleeveless red T-shirt with the face of an angry serial killer or a dead revolutionary, hard to tell, no real difference, a tat on his left arm, ragged jeans, boots, I shout back, you're too old for emo, and goth is so last century

I dropped out of school, he says, those guys, they arent me, can we talk, can we go somewhere?

I fumble for my keys, he's got a knapsack hung over his left shoulder, he follows me to the door

outside in the dry night, my eyes ache, I blink against the street lights, last time we were both here, it was bloody, there were bodies flying, I dont know if I have the strength for that anymore, maybe I never did, but I did it anyway, but now I'm feeling my age, I find my keys, he snatches them out of my hand, you're in no shape to drive

and you are?

I dont drink, he opens the passenger door for me, waits till I climb in, goes around to the driver side

we sit for a bit, not talking, maybe he's trying to figure out what to say, finally I ask, we going somewhere?

"What did you do to me?" he demands, angry. "I've got all this shit in my head. Memories. Faces. Pieces of other people's lives. People I dont know! I dont know who I am anymore—"

you never knew who you were, nobody does, did I say that out loud

"Shut the fuck up. You did something, Chase—"

first time anyone's used my name in years, I've been called a lot of things, but

"*Something happened.* You were there too! What was it? What did you do to me?"

I open my mouth to say something, close it, shake my head

"It doesn't stop!" he says. "There's this girl—she's

crying about something, I dont know what, but every so often, I'm her. Or she's me. I'm not sure what she's crying about. I think she's trying to kill herself, but she's afraid. And there's this little boy, there's something wrong inside his head, I can feel it, I can't explain it, he doesn't understand what's happening around him, all the strange people who keep coming and going. And there's this old man, he has a secret, he did something terrible, something he can't tell anyone, and I'm starting to know his secret too—and it's awful, I dont want to know it, people were hurt, they died, he still hears them screaming. And there's—" He stops abruptly, takes a deep breath, an intake of resolve, stares into my face, eyes probing, demanding. "You know what it is, dont you? Tell me what *happened*—?"

I cant, it's not that I dont want to, but I cant, I dont know what to say—another frustrated shake, not angry, exasperated—there aren't any words for it

"Who are all these people—why are they in my head? Or am I in theirs? It's happening more and more. I bounce from one life to another, flashing through them like some deranged montage that doesn't make any sense. I've been—" Long pause, longer, he struggles inside, fighting to form the words. "You dont know what I've been through, Chase. I've been raped. And I've been the rapist too. I've killed people—and I've been murdered. I've given birth. I've been the baby—I've nursed myself at my own chest. Sometimes I'm alone, sometimes I'm in a crowd. I'm walking in the dark or down a bright corridor. I'm locked in a cell. I'm falling through space. And sometimes—" His expression is haunted. "—sometimes, I'm being fucked. Or fucking. Or on my knees—I've been men, I've been women, and twice I've been children. I've been in bed with men, with women, with—you cant imagine, once even with a dog—" His eyes are wide with terror, speaking it aloud to another person, sharing it, the words finally make it real.

"At first I thought these were some kind of I dont know, delusions or something, not real, just very real hallucinations, but every time it *happened*, I felt it more and more intensely. Until I couldn't deny the truth of it anymore. I thought I was losing myself—going insane. But then one night, and this one was so vivid, I wasn't me anymore, I was—I was this skinny little boy, or maybe a girl, I wasn't sure, the room was dimly lit, red lamps, gold and yellow walls, but you were there, you were naked, you were on your back and you were a lot younger, you still had both your legs, I was straddling you, and you were inside me and we were, we were—" He didn't want to finish the sentence. He said something else instead. "—but that's when I knew I wasn't going crazy. That's when I knew it was all about you. You did something to me, didn't you?"

shake my head—no, I didnt, yeah it *happened*, but I didnt

He doesn't believe me. "Fuck you! You're lying! You know what this is! I need to know. You have to tell me! What's going on? What is this? Why am I being all these other people? And what am I supposed to do with all this—all this crap piling up in my head? And—and even more important, Chase, tell me—how the fuck do I make it stop?"

I wish I knew

"But you know something—!"

I know when it started, that's all

"I want you to tell me. Everything!"

so we end up driving, somewhere, anywhere, and end up sitting on a stone bench in an empty lawn, in the middle of a place that might be a college campus or a park or a place in the middle of limbo, we're in the shadows away from the lights, one of those places where men come to do things with other men, and that's what we're about to do, only not quite the same thing, something much more intimate than just yanking each other off

Michael—his name is Michael—he hands me a bottle of water from his knapsack, I pop it open and drink, I look at him, a question in my eyes, it's a long story

he says he doesnt mind, I've been living with this too long, now I've found you again, you're going to tell me, tell me everything you know

yeah, okay, I'll tell you, but you wont like it—you'll hate it and you'll be pissed at me for dropping it into your lap, you know that thing they say, once it's been seen, it cant be unseen—well, this is the only warning you're going to get, you want to quit now, speak up

he shakes his head, I'm not quitting, "It cant be worse than what I'm already experiencing."

yeah? you think so?

"I just want to clean all this shit out of my head!"

yeah, that's not possible, see there's this thing I know, I learned it when I was washing dishes and mopping floors, bussing tables and cleaning up after the pigs who thought the whole world was their sty—there's no such thing as cleaning, there's just moving the dirt around from one place to another, really, we'd scrape it off the tables and put it in a plastic bag, and then we'd put the plastic bags in a dumpster, and then the big green truck would roll up and empty the dumpster into its back, and drive out somewhere on the other side of the hills and empty itself there, like a bear shitting in the woods, only this was more like a titanosaur, because it was taking the biggest dump of all, a couple tons at a time, call it a ti*ton*osaur maybe, but there would be all that shit, all that crap, all piled up in one big place, and we would pretend we had cleaned something, but all we had done is create one big toxic mountain of it, all compressed and concentrated, all in one place, slowly decaying, decomposing, and leaching its various poisons into the ground, into the soil, into the water, right back into our lives, so we didnt really clean anything at all, we just squeezed it all into a big piece of karmic spite that would come back to us as asthma and allergies, and then cancer and lung disease, and crap knows what else

and human beings—we're like that too, we think we're cleaning out our heads, we spew our hate and our fear and our anger at each other, we think we're getting rid of it, no, no, no, all we're doing is giving it away, putting it into the next person's head, and apparently we have an endless supply of bullshit to pass around and share

you know I thought about suicide once—Michael looks amazed, he blinks, he says, "You? Really? You're the toughest person I know," and I say, "I wish I was as tough as you think, I wish, I was just too big a coward to kill myself." Shrug. "Later on—a long time later on, when I finally had to tell the truth about it, when I could finally look at it from outside, from above, from the peyote-clarity of the desert, when I finally got free of all the stories and all the conversations I'd been carrying around—no, I didnt get free, there is no free, but I recognized they were part of my past, not part of any future I wanted to have, so all that shit, it had no power except what I gave it by endlessly rehearsing it, and after everything else, I fell out of that cycle, it was obvious how stupid suicide would have been. I mean, forever is a long time to go away, and—and see, here's the big realization, it wouldnt have made any difference to me at the time, but it was important for me to realize it later on. I wouldnt have been making the pain go away, I'd have just been passing it on to someone else—to whoever had to clean up the body maybe. Or maybe my family. Or I dont know. But it's like all the other dirt. You think you're cleaning, but you're not. You're just moving it around. And that's not fair to the other guy, the person you dump it on.

Michael doesnt answer right away. When he does, his voice is almost a whisper. Embarrassed. "I think you're tough...."

yeah, now. Maybe. But the truth? I'm the biggest fucking sissy you'll ever meet in your life. Yeah, I know, you see this great hulking bear, or what's left of one, so you assume—that's what you all do, you assume, you dont ask—you want to know the truth? My mom didnt want to be bothered anymore, I was an accident, a surprise, she only wanted two, she got three, she was already exhausted from the first two, they werent easy kids to raise either, maybe that was her fault, she was a screamer, we all learned to scream back because we thought that's what families did, and maybe that's just more bullshit, I dont know—what I do know is that she couldnt wait to get me out of the house, I heard her say so more than once, she was always on the phone complaining to whoever would listen, so I learned how to be alone from the beginning—anyway, even though the minimum enrollment age was five, she lied and pushed me into kindergarten when I was four and a half, so I was already six months out of sync with everyone else, and I was the smallest and the smartest and you know how that works out, more so the older you get, and it wasnt any better at home, because my brother and my sister didnt want to be baby-sitters, they were already teenagers and I was the nuisance brat—even worse, I was a sissy—

Michael looks at me, startled again that I used the word.

yeah, Michael, yeah. I'm not ashamed of it. I was the best sissy in the world. I put on my mother's makeup, I put on my sister's dresses, she thought it was cute, she gave me her hand-me-downs and

I'd play dress-up, wearing her panties and slips and sleeping in her old nightgowns, and I liked it 'cause it felt good against my skin, my mother pretended it was all a game, all a phase, until she started seeing this guy who said it was queer and he was going to beat it out of me, make a man out of me, and he did that every time he came home drunk, which was every night—and yeah, I know this is a familiar story, you've already heard it enough times to be bored with it, but that doesnt make it any less true—

and growing up—the smallest and the smartest again, right?—the kids at school called me sissy, punched me every time they passed, dropped me in trash cans, pushed me into lockers, shoved my head into the toilet, gave me swirlies, pantsed me, beat me up, made me the school joke, and even the teachers—the fucking teachers—they'd say crap like, "Well, you brought it on yourself. If you'd just stop being such a sissy, they wouldnt beat you up"—do you know how stupid that sounds to a kid who's already bruised and battered and hurting and just wants to be left alone—

and then I'd go home and the guy who would have been my step-dad if my mom had married him, only he didnt want to get pinned down, he was happy to have free meals and free fucks—no, that's not fair, he threw some money at her once in a while, told her to fix herself up because she looked like a pig, and if she wanted him to fuck her, she should at least try to look like a woman, if he wanted to fuck a man he said he could fuck me, I was already fourteen when he said that and he'd been beating me up for so long, I was one gigantic bruise and I didnt care anymore, next thing I knew, I'd punched him in the balls, I'd missed, I was aiming for his big fat gut, but I'd missed because I was still too short and he was tall enough to touch the ceiling just by reaching up, but my punch landed right in his balls and he doubled over with a grunt because I'd hit him just in the right place, so hard he couldnt think of anything except grabbing himself, and my older brother who was visiting, he fell on the floor laughing, 'ha ha, the sissy beat you up,' and then I dont know what happened next or how, except I was on top of the bastard, punching him like I never punched anything before, and I hadnt—so I dont know how I knew how to punch him, but I was punching and punching and punching, his face and his throat and all over his head, with my little fists—except I was wearing my sister's junk jewelry rings, the big heavy ones with lots of pointy bits, and he was bleeding like a sponge, every punch was another squeeze—and finally my mother was on top of me, trying to pull me off, slapping me on my back and sides and screeching like a fucking banshee, calling me all kinds of words, mostly incoherent—and when she finally fell on top of me, squashing me like a bug under a great sweaty blob, I couldnt move, and when the bear underneath rolled us both off, he just looked at us and didnt know which one to hit first, he started in on me, and then my brother threw himself at him, screaming for him to leave me alone, hadnt he done enough damage and I think that was the first time he'd ever stood up for me anywhere—he said, pick on someone your own size for a change, so the bastard started punching my brother, only my brother was in pretty good shape, from all that football, and he put the bastard up against the wall, and then my mom was screaming "no, no, no, stop it, stop it," and she was waving a kitchen knife and I dont think she knew who she was going to attack, she just started waving and slashing at everything like a crazy woman, there was a lot of blood everywhere—

and when the police finally arrived and the paramedics too, everyone was bleeding and somebody tried to scoop me up, wrap a blanket around me, put me in an ambulance because I must have looked like a horror story, and I kept shouting and screaming, no, no, no, no, leave me alone, leave me alone, dont touch me, dont touch me—and there was this lady paramedic, a black lady, and she just stood in front of me staring into my eyes, I remember her eyes, big and brown, telling me it's all right, it's all right, sweetie, what's your name, what's your name, nobody's going to hurt you, nobody's going to touch you, and I started shouting at her, "Yes, I am a fucking sissy, I know it, everybody always says it, all the kids at school, my brother, that man who fucks my mom, my mom says it too, it's like they think I dont know it, I have to be reminded, well I dont—I dont need to be told again, I know I'm a sissy, so just leave me alone, leave me the fuck alone already—"

but she wouldn't, no—she reached over and took my hands in hers and said, "Listen to me, sweetie. Sissies are some of the strongest people in the world, maybe the very strongest. I never met a sissy who wasnt so tough, nothing could hurt him."

"Bullshit, bullshit, bullshit. Everything hurts. And nobody cares, nobody, nobody, nobody. Not the bastard, not my mom, not my brother, nobody—"

"I care," she said. "And your brother cares, doesnt he? He stopped your dad from hurting you, didn't he?"

"He's not my dad, he's just the guy who fucks my mom. He's just the guy who eats all our food and beats me up—"

"But you beat him up tonight, didn't you?"

I started crying. "I only punched him in the balls."

"But it stopped him, didn't it?"

"It just hurt so much. All the time. Every day. Everybody calls me sissy. Why doesnt anyone like me—?"

"I like you," she said. "You're the bravest sissy I've ever met. You hit him back."

"That's not brave," I said. "I was angry, so angry I couldnt help myself—"

"Listen to me," she said. "Listen good, listen hard.

You dont know it yet, but you will, someday. One day, somebody's going to say something mean to you and you're going to look at him and say, 'Is that all? Is that the best you got? I heard worse from my gramma.'"

I wiped my nose on my sleeve. It came away bloody. But I stopped sniffling and looked at her.

"One day," she said. "One day, it doesn't matter what life throws at you. You'll say, 'Is that the best you got? Take your best shot. I've already been through the worst the universe can throw at me and I'm still here. I'm still standing. There's nothing you can do—you can't touch me.'"

"You're making that up."

"No, I'm not. Look at the color of my skin, honey. I grew up in Alabama. I bet you can still hear it in my voice, can't you? You think I dont know? Nobody's born tough. You learn it from everybody around you—they're teaching you something important."

I mumbled something, I dont remember, it wasnt coherent. Something about, "I dont want to be a sissy anymore. I just want to die."

She pushed my chin up so I had to look at her and she said, "No, you're not. You're not going to waste your life. You're going to grow up to be tougher than everybody. This is the day it starts." She squeezed my hands gently. "Are you ready? I'm going to tell you the secret—and as long as you remember this, nobody can make you feel bad about yourself ever again. You ready?"

I nodded.

"You listen good now, honey. You listen powerful good. It doesn't matter what people say to you. It doesn't matter what awful names they call you or what terrible things they tell you about yourself—they're not talking about you at all. They're telling you about themselves. They're telling you what they're afraid of, what they're angry about, what they're missing inside themselves, what they want and are too scared to reach for. They're telling you everything that's wrong with them. Dont you never never ever forget that."

I swallowed hard. Nodded. "Okay."

"Okay." She looked deep into me. "Can I clean you up now? Can I see if you're hurt anywhere else?"

I didnt say anything for a long time, that was the important part of the story and there wasnt anything more to add, but finally Michael had to ask, "So, um, what happened? I mean after that night?"

shrug

nobody got arrested, the cops didnt want to bother, but the asshole went away and never came back, maybe they gave him a choice, go to jail or go away, it wasnt the first time they'd been called out, but it was the worst time—whatever it was, it was better than before, but after a while, my mom started blaming me for him leaving, only the way she told it I was the reason she couldnt keep a man, because what real man wanted to be around a sissy all the time, and I dont know when it started or how or why, but one day I just started sassing back. I said to her, "Whynt you just buy a vibrator? It's cheaper and it wont steal money out of your purse for beer."

adolescence is where you wrestle with your sexuality, I wrestled with mine every night, usually two or three times, and the best times were when I let myself wrestle with fantasies of other boys, other men—no, I didnt know the details of what we might do or how we might do it, I just knew that we would do it together, probably naked, just holding onto each other, and that was when I began to figure it out, this is what I like, so this is who I am—so if I'm gonna be a sissy, I'm gonna be a good one, I'm gonna be the biggest baddest sassiest sissy of all—you want to fuck with me, I'm gonna fuck right back—because it aint rape if you fuck back

fifteen, maybe sixteen, certainly by seventeen, I learned how to be a bitch, a really nasty foul-mouthed, dont fuck with me fellas, beeyotch, and it lasted until—well, I'll tell you about that in a minute, but I went through, I dont know, call it a phase, but I was good at it

you dont know this about queerboys, nobody does, except maybe other queerboys who survived it, but we didnt exist in the real world, we were invisible, there weren't any role models—not then—nothing in the movies, nothing on TV, nothing in the news except drag queens and suicides and people dying of plague. Everywhere else, everyone, people are saying shit like, "Be yourself" and "Grab life by the throat" and "Seize the moment"—but you know what they were saying to queer kids? Nothing useful. Nobody was saying, "You can have a life too." Nobody was saying, "It gets better," then—you know why? Because it never gets better for queerkids. You just get older and it gets worse. If you survive, you get stronger, but that's only if you survive—so, no we didnt know who we were or who we were supposed to be, and not even a hint of who we could be if we wanted to be anything at all—and if we wanted to be anything, we had to hide the most important part of ourselves, or...or nothing

so—this is what happened, little Michael. This is who we turned into instead. Once we admitted to ourselves that we liked boys, we turned into girls, silly little girls. We didnt get our adolescence in high school like everyone else, we didnt get to hold hands, have a first kiss, or a real date, we were all in hiding from each other, from ourselves most of all, so we had to make it up somewhere else, this was it, puberty reinvented in our own images, so yeah, Michael, we didnt just come out of the closet, we exploded out of it in fabulous fabulous clothes, and fabulous fabulous shoes and fabulous fabulous makeup and everything else, so if people were going to call us faggots and fairies and sissies, we were going to wear it like rhinestones and dance till fucking dawn—you know why I did it? Because it drove everyone crazy. My sister, my brother, they rolled their eyes, but after a while they laughed it off, but my mother, especially my mother, she couldnt handle it, she went the whole nine yards of crazy batshit. I'd put on a purple anything and that would enough to set her off, or she'd see me trying on one of my sister's discarded old tops, the one with all the sequins and lace, and she'd start screaming, I'd just flutter my eyelashes at her and say, "You're just mad because this looks better on me than it does on you." And it did, we both knew it—

and you want to know something, Michael? The more sissy I got, the worse everybody else got—everywhere I went, people would shout stuff at me. And I made up my mind to be meaner and nastier than all of them rolled together. A woman on the street stops and looks at me, gives me the hate stare, she says, "What are you? Some kind of faggot?" And I look at her, I look her up and down, I wrinkle my nose and curl my lip like I just smelled something awful, and I say, "Are *you* the alternative?" It was worth it to see her eyes go wide—

another time, any time, it doesnt matter when, somebody shouts, "homo" from their car and I turn and wave wildly and laugh and smile and shout right back, 'Thank you, honey! Thank you for noticing! I am fabulous tonight.' What can they say? What can they do? The black lady was right, they cant touch me, it was a start, but it was enough, I didnt have to hurt anymore, they did—

yeah, Michael, it's hard to believe I know, but I wasnt born old, I had to get here the old-fashioned way, one day at a time, you said you wanted to know, well this is it, this is the rest of it, this is everything, so shut up and listen—because I wasnt just a sissy, I was *the* sissy. I was the best sissy. I was the standard by which all other sissies had to be measured, at least until—okay, I said I'd tell you about the until, this is it—until one night I'm fabulously flaunting flouncing my way down the street and a carload of boys screeches to a stop right next to me and they tumble out so fast, it's like the clown car at a circus, except there's nothing funny about these clowns, they're all over me so fast, kicking and punching and screaming, "faggot" and "queer" and all the other words I'd been so proud of just two minutes before, and all I can do is roll into a ball with my hands over my head, while they're kicking and shouting and for a minute I'm realizing, "oh my god, I'm going to die" and at the same time thinking oh shit, mom is going to love this, I could already see her shaking her head, if she came to the hospital at all—

and then there's some more screaming and shouting and banging, I dont know what happened next, I couldnt see, the blood was streaming down into my eyes, and then there's a screech of tires and a bang, the sound of one car slamming into another, so maybe they didnt get away after all, except there's another screech and they're gone and a whole bunch of people are shouting, but I'm still on the ground, waiting for the pain to kick in, and I've peed myself, maybe shit my pants, or maybe it's blood, I dont know—

okay, so somebody drives me to the hospital, the emergency room, and at first none of the doctors even want to see me, you know what I'm hearing? "Well, he brought it on himself—" like I fucking walked down the street with a big "Kick Me" sign on my back. Yeah, I'm a sissy, I know it, what am I supposed to do, pretend I'm not? But when did that give anyone permission to kick the shit out of me? But there's some guy on the other side of the curtain, he's yelling at someone else that if they dont treat me, and treat me now, there's gonna be reporters and lawyers all over this place like you wont believe, you think I dont know how to make trouble for you, you little pissant, that's a teenage boy in there, and you get in there and you fix him up or I'm gonna put you in worse shape than he is—

and I dont know who the guy screaming is, but I'm really starting to like him, even though I can barely breathe, I'm coughing up blood and I've got a pain in my side like broken glass, and it turns out when they finally do X-ray me, I've got a broken rib and it's punctured a lung, and next thing I'm being wheeled into an operating room, all white and bright, and when I wake up again, there's a big bearded guy, he looks like a biker, because he's all tattoos, and where there arent any tattoos, there's hair—he's sitting next to my bed and as soon as I open my eyes, even before I finish focusing, he leans down to whisper, "My name is Max. If they ask, tell them I'm your brother. That's what I told them. Play along, otherwise they wont let me back in—" I dont know who this guy is, but he's already done more for me in one night than my real brother, maybe not, I dont know, by then I havent seen my real brother in a year, I havent seen anyone in my family, I'm living in an abandoned house a bunch of us are using as a commune when we're not turning tricks—yeah, didnt I mention that? Survival sex, look it up. Only at least, guys were paying me for what I wanted to do anyway.

so there I was, Michael, a nineteen year old street-rat, fresh out of high school—yeah, I did finish high school, I was too mean or too stubborn or too stupid to quit—and I was going to get out of my mother's house as fast as I could, so there I was, selling my scrawny little eighteen/nineteen year-old body to every so-called straight guy who didnt want his wife to know he still liked cock, and oh yeah, you wouldnt believe how many of those guys there are, I made a lot of money off them—the difference between me and them? I dont pretend to be something I'm not. I'm the honest sissy—

Max, my new brother tells me I'm going to be okay, but it'll take a while—he goes on to explain that the boys who beat me were amateurs, they didnt know how to go for the bad parts. Somebody got their license number, turned them in for a hit-and-run, but somebody's daddy must have opened his checkbook to fix the other car because the police didnt go after them, and nothing was said about the bashing either, such was the police, in those days we pronounced it po-lice.

I still havent said a word, he looks at me, he asks, "Can I be serious?" Me, I can only be funny and sarcastic in response, because that's all I've ever learned how to be, so I say, "I dunno, can you?" And he says, "Okay, let's do it your way. Shut up and listen. I had a little brother, just like you—very much like you, every bit as fabulous and every bit as stupid, and he's dead now, just like you would have been if I hadnt been there to stop them. I wasnt there for my little brother and I didnt know how much I loved him until he was gone and I couldnt tell him, he never knew, he died thinking he was alone and nobody cared and I've hated myself every day since then, but maybe I can do something for you and maybe I can make up for my own mistake a little bit."

yeah, that's all very sad, I said, but what's that got to do with me. So, he holds up my hand in front of my face, so I have to look at my purple glitter nail-polish, and he says, "You. Do. Not. Have. To. Do. This." And I say right back to him, as nasty as I can, "Oh, yeah? What else can I do? Who else can I be?" And he says, "Anyone you want. So why did you choose this?"

yeah? What else was there? I'm a sissy. That's

all I can be. That's all anybody ever let me be. So I might as well be a big sissy, the biggest. And he says right back to me, "That's what my stupid little brother said to me too." He leans in, he grabs me by the throat, not my shirt, my throat—it was already painful to breathe, what with the cracked lungs and the tape and everything else—and he says, "If you've got enough strength to be a sissy, you've got enough strength to be anything else you want," and I say right back to him, "well, what if I want to be a sissy?" and he stares down into my face and he says, "yeah, and how's that working for you?" And he's got me there. "Having a little trouble breathing?" He lets go. "You want to look in the mirror? Purple is your color today. Tomorrow or the next day, it'll be yellow. You like this? There are a lot of other guys out there willing to keep you in purple and yellow." And I'll tell you the truth, Michael, I didnt answer him right then—partly because it hurt too much to speak and partly because I knew he was right, I was going to get beaten up a lot. I coulda said, "okay, yeah, help me." I shoulda said it, but I was too full of anger and hatred and everything else. I was too full of myself—or something of equally squishy consistency

so I was an asshole. I just looked up at Max and told him to go to hell, go away, get the fuck out of my life, I dont need any hairy-bear do-gooder trying to salve his conscience on me. So he can take his pseudo-quasi-phony Tom-of-Finland tough guy act off to Silverlake or maybe up to Folsom street, which I'd only heard of, never been there, where he might find someone else who wants to believe in it, not me, and if he wants anything else from me, he can pay for it, just like everybody else. The only thing that's free is a penguin—that's where you drop your pants, I give you a couple yanks and then walk away bored, and you waddle after me, saying, "hey, wait! Is that all there is?" Yeah, that's all there is.

after he left, as soon as I could, I got out of bed, I washed my face real good, I still had mascara and glitter, I wet my hair and flattened it, I found my clothes and somehow managed to dress myself and walked out of that place. I caught a bus back to the crash pad, only nobody was there, the cops had chased everybody out, so I slept out in the back on an old collapsed porch swing that nobody had ever gotten around to hauling away

and I'm laying there in the dark, curled up like a baby, too cold to sleep, trying not to cry and crying anyway, thinking of killing myself again, wishing I hadnt told Max to fuck off, wishing I'd stayed where it was warm, wishing I wasnt such a pussy, wishing I could get even with those assholes who busted my ribs, wishing I could fuck them in the ass with a rabid porcupine, wishing I could just have something nice for a change, and cursing out God for everything, for making me this way—I mean, I tried to change, I did, everybody tries to change, Michael. Not just the queerboys. You look in the mirror and all you see is what's wrong, I'm not *this* enough or I'm not *that* enough, and you spend your whole life trying to fix yourself, because you just want to be okay inside your head, you know?

I know you know this, Michael, that's why you're here. You're looking for the fix. Yeah, that's why they call it a fix. Because you think you're broken. Only you're not—that broken feeling? That's normal. That's how you know you're normal. If you're not feeling it, you really are broken, that's the joke

and maybe it wasnt that day or the next, but I started wrapping myself around my anger, using it to keep warm at first, then later on, using it as a weapon. If you'd thought I was a nasty little sissy before, that was nothing compared to what I was turning into—I was turning into the royal bitch-queen, and that's when I started to get dangerous—I mean, really dangerous. Because somewhere in there I made up my mind, as God is my witness, or whatever imaginary companion anyone wants to believe in, as God is my fucking witness, the next time I'm in a fight, win or lose, the other guy is gonna know he's been in a fucking fight—the next time I come home with blood on my hands, it's gonna be someone else's

I didnt know how I was going to get from anywhere to there, but I finally had a—a vision, a picture in my head of what I wanted to be. I wanted to be so fucking dangerous, nobody would ever touch me again unless I wanted them to. And on my terms, Michael. On my terms.

Michael stopped me because my voice was cracking—he passed me the water bottle and I drank until I coughed. I would have waved him away but I was coughing too hard, nothing wrong with me, just the night air

in the movies, you run into the dark forest, as far as you can, until you find a cute little house where seven little men or a kindly old woman who wishes she had a child are just waiting to wrap you into their lives—and the birds and mice will help you clean and even fix up a new dress for you, and everybody's singing and dancing and having a wonderful time—

in real life, it's cold and dark and hungry, and all seven of those little men just want to get your panties off you and—so having an idea and making it happen—there's this thing in the way called reality, which is mostly time and money and sometimes even ability. Remember, I was still just a skinny little fairy. Inside, I still am. Sometimes I amaze myself how far this little faggot has come. Dont flinch, Michael. I own these words, they're mine. They cant hurt me.

anyway, one of the places I was taking tricks was

a bath house on Melrose, I think it was on Melrose, maybe it was on Santa Monica, I dont remember. A lot of stuff has gotten knocked loose inside this old head since then, but it was a place for old men—by old, I mean men who were as old as I am now, but when you're nineteen, that's ancient. They'd bring me there and fuck me or suck me or sometimes just lay on top of me and pretend they were getting it up. The owners knew what I was doing, they didnt care, not as long as I was bringing in customers and staying discreet about it. Discreet, hah—that's another form of the closet. Dont flaunt it. Dont call attention to yourself—

no, I was never out there marching or shouting or getting political. I didnt see the sense in it. Nothing was going to change. Why vote? Yeah, I see the look on your face, do you see the look on mine? Where I was, down at the bottom—no, underneath the bottom—I wasnt getting anything, no matter who was on top. They all looked like posers to me, puffed up in their white shirts and silk suits in their various offices in the daytime, but after dark—they were just another trick, pulling their Beemer or their Mercedes over to the curb to give me that look, that once over, and then if they liked what they saw—the skinny kid scowling in a T-shirt and tight jeans—they'd nod and I'd stroll over to their open car window and I'd lean down so they could get a look at me and maybe decide if they were that hungry to get off and if I'd be able to buy something to eat afterward

they'd say stupid things like, "Where's it happening?" Or, "Need a ride?" Anything to look innocent. The guys who knew the game, they came right out and said it, "Wanna party?" And I'd say, "Tell me you're not a cop," because they werent allowed to lie about it, but they did anyway—but I wouldnt talk money or anything until I got in the car and we drove across La Brea, the invisible dividing line between the city and the county. This was when West Hollywood wasnt incorporated, so the city cops couldnt cross the line and arrest you in there, only the Sheriff's deputies could, only the deputies wouldnt arrest you, they'd just beat you up—

okay, yeah—that was one of the political things, I did get involved. I did show up at the protests. It took years, but eventually, we got the police and the deputies to stop bashing us, we're citizens too—okay, yeah, we're hustlers and junkies and queers, but some of us pay taxes and we deserve, I dunno, is it too much to ask, that the cops who are supposed to protect us not be the ones beating on us? Especially because some of you guys are taking us out behind the bushes up in Griffith Park sometimes. Yeah, they were—and they werent always paying for it either. A free blow job, that was one of the perks when you serve and protect. And I can tell you something about that too—

in those days, you could get twenty, maybe thirty bucks. Not a lot, but gas was only fifty cents a gallon, and you could get a couple of shitburgers and fries for less than a buck at McFuck's. That's what we called it. There were these do-gooders that came around, they called us "youth at risk" and they wanted to get us off the streets, they were as bad as the cops and the marks—they were the good gays, they said, but they wanted the same thing—they wanted us, I could tell, because we were young and they werent anymore

oh yeah, they talked to us about how many of us would end up as junkies—and how many of us would end up dead before we were thirty, like we could even imagine thirty. Suicide didnt scare me, I'd already looked into that abyss—I knew I'd go there someday, I just had to finish working up the courage, but not until I got even, not until I punched in a few faces. And then there was Max again, the hairy-bear, he knew me, I pretended I didnt remember him, he said I was too smart for this shit. He said one day maybe some trick wouldnt just beat me up when he was done, maybe he'd pull a knife and slash my throat. They were finding bodies up in the hills or alongside the freeways, did I want to be a statistic? He thought he was going to scare me—

okay, anyway—lemme have more water, please. Yeah, thanks. Anyway, when I did have money in my jeans, when I didnt want to be pawed over—

okay, wait. Wait. Here's the part nobody ever tells you. It wasnt all bad. Some of it was... sometimes, it was nice. There was this one guy, I saw him a few times. His name was Joe and he worked at one of the studios, I think, he drove a white Cougar convertible, always with the top down, he didnt care who saw him. Maybe he was twenty-nine or thirty, he looked young, even younger than that, like another kid, but he had a job and he had money. If he saw me, he'd pull over and pick me up, we'd go out to his place, somewhere in the valley, I think it was Studio City, not the hills, the flats where they had all these weird little bungalows and duplexes and guest houses. He must have been making some real bucks, he had a king size water bed and he'd give me a hundred bills just to spend the night with him, usually more, like he was really grateful to be with me. He wasnt kinky, mostly it was plain vanilla, occasionally a little chocolate, but mostly he just wanted someone to hold him and kiss him and roll with him and pretend to care, and yeah, if I'd have been a different person, if he hadnt been stuffing twenties into my shirt pocket in the morning, yeah, I coulda cared. You know why? Because he respected me. He didnt treat me like a piece of crap. He listened to me, he laughed when I said something funny, and he wrinkled up his face in hurt when I said something painful—like when he asked me about this scar across my ribs.

He touched it, traced it with his fingertips, you know, and said something nobody had ever said before. He said it gave me character. He said it was evidence I was living life hard. At first I thought he was going to give me some bullshit like how it was evidence that I could get back up when I was knocked down, but he didnt. Instead, he said he was jealous of me, of all I'd seen and done and been through. He said he'd grown up in a neighborhood so white bread you could smear mayonnaise on it and make a baloney sandwich. He said he was living in the pillow-world—where it didnt matter how hard you threw yourself at the walls, you werent going to get hurt. Like riding in a big pink bubble with Glinda the Good. You wanna notice, Glinda was the real bitch, she never got her hands dirty, but everybody else got killed or sent home, leaving her the head honcho in Oz. If I could be anybody, I'd be Glinda, fruity pink dress and all—clean and pretty, and a take-no-prisoners bitch. But here was Joe, with his soft soft hands and his soft soft body and his very hard cock and he'd look into my eyes and tell me how strong I was, and he meant it, and he said he always wondered if he could ever be as strong as me if the time came when he had to

he'd hold me close all night long and sometimes we'd do it again in the morning, and then he'd fix us a little breakfast, a big breakfast if it was a weekend, eggs and bacon and strawberries, but if it was a weekday and he had to go to work, he'd just make coffee and toast, and then drop me somewhere convenient on his way to Paramount or wherever. He didnt have to do that, but he did it anyway, and it meant a lot, it meant I was a real person to him. He said he liked doing things for me, I think it's because he got to be the strong one in bed, I made him be the strong one. I think he just liked feeling in control of his own life, I dont know what kind of job he had, he said he couldnt talk about it, but he didnt always look happy driving in. I could see him getting smaller and smaller inside. But with me—he was, okay, I wont say alive, because I didnt know then what it was to be alive, but with me, he was better. And so was I. I was always happy to see his white Cougar come cruising down the street, because I knew I was going to have a nice night. I dont think he picked up anyone else after he started seeing me. He asked me for my phone number, but I didnt have one. Some of the guys had answering services, but I didnt want to spend the money.

he wasnt a rescuer, I didnt want him to be, but if he'd ever said, 'I want you to stay with me,' I would have. And not just because it would have been easy, or free. But because he was nice, he never asked me for anything I didnt already want to give to him. We had fun. Not like a lot of other guys, but yeah, that part was fun. I'd have done him for free, I even told him that once, but he said no and gave me an extra hundred. He said he knew it had to be hard to survive on the streets. He said, just once, but I remembered it, that I was too good for the street, too enthusiastic. Ha! I told him I loved my job, not a lot of people can say that, can they? That made him laugh. But sometimes I wonder if he'd been about to suggest I stay with him for awhile, go back to school, anything—

okay, so it wasnt always that nice. Sometimes it was ugly. And sometimes I took a day off and went to the beach with—well, I cant call them friends, but that's what they looked like at the time. I guess you'd call it a "mental health day" now. We'd get on the bus and we'd start camping it up, flaming away, having our own little party—we were already drunk and/or stoned before we got on, so we didnt care. But we still had to be careful. Sometimes the bus driver would get so pissed at us, he'd make us get off wherever we were, and some of those neighborhoods were very blue collar, not too safe for a gaggle of little princesses. No, I wasnt a queen, not yet. My mother was still alive. I saw her on holidays. Especially my birthday and Christmas, she'd give me a card and a check for twenty-five bucks, a kiss on the cheek and "go buy something nice for yourself, honey," but you're not a real queen until a prince marries you and carries you off to rule his kingdom for him, while he was out chasing dragons. Me, I wanted to be the Red Queen with my own little stable of tarts and twinkies. I wanted to be able to bellow, "Off with his head!" when someone pissed me off, and it wasnt gonna be the big head I was talking about

but when I had money in my pocket, even a little, and I just wanted to be alone, I'd go to the tubs—that's what we called it. It was another bath house, but this one was only for kids, you had to be eighteen at least, and you had to be brought by someone who was already a member. It was owned by a guy named Scotty. Maybe he was in his thirties or forties. You'd go in through a little foyer, Scotty sat behind the glass, you'd pay two or three bucks to go in, I dont remember, but it was cheap enough. You'd go in, you'd rent a locker or if you had an extra buck, you'd rent a room, you'd take off all your clothes, wrap a towel around your waist, and you were ready. You had to fold the towel lengthwise so it would show more, otherwise you looked like, I dunno, a straight guy who didnt know where he was. But this was our place, a place where being homosexual wasnt just accepted, it was required, no—it was beyond that, this was a place where the rest of the world didnt exist, there werent any straight boys anymore. Everyone here was here for the same reason. We all liked cock. Our own. Each other's. But here's the thing that nobody who wasnt there can understand. It wasnt about the sex. Yeah, you could have sex, but you didnt go just for the sex. You went there to be safe. You could shower and shave, you could watch TV, have some snacks, you could go up on the roof and sunbathe or moonbathe if it was night, the neighbors in the nearby apartments apparently enjoyed the view—or you could just go to a room and sleep it off, until whenever you finally revived. And sometimes, you could sit and have a Coke with another queerboy and just talk about stuff without anything else being on the table, those were the best nights

the tubs were a lot cheaper than a motel and a lot more fun, there was a workout room and a hot tub and yeah, okay, there was no shortage of sex if that's what you were there for. You could wander the halls for a while, all the light bulbs were red, I figure if there really is a hell that's what it's going to look like—everyone wandering up one hall and down the next, wandering until you found someone who's willing to hold onto you while you hump yourself against them, and if you didnt find anyone you could still go into the orgy room, which was all black-light and blue. There werent always guys doing it, but sometimes when the place got busy, there were three or four at a time. I learned a lot, just watching. Funny thing, I wasnt interested in orgies. I wanted one-on-one. I wanted, yeah, call it a delusion, I wanted the delusion of love, even if it was only for a few humpy minutes. But I should tell you about the rooms, they werent really rooms, just partitioned off places with beaten-up mattresses on the floor, maybe raised up on wooden pallets, I dont remember, and the partitions were so thin you couldnt lean on them without them creaking, and they all had holes in them—glory holes, yeah—but also convenient for peeking, for watching what was going on in the next room over, but usually it was pretty boring stuff, most sex is boring unless you're doing it yourself, that's how I felt about it, although sometimes I saw some things that made me think I should try that if I find the right guy

but all in all, it was a nice place, nicer than most places I'd been, up to that time, because all the guys had passed the Scotty test. See, if Scotty didnt like a guy you'd brought, someone who didnt have a membership card yet, he'd say, 'Sorry, we're not having a membership night tonight, no guests.' That was code for, 'This one's a troll. Dont bring trolls here, okay?' But if Scotty liked your looks, if he thought you were cute enough, he'd give you a card and let you in on the Scotty code. So yeah, when I needed to get away, I went to Scotty's. I'm pretty sure this one was on Melrose. The official name was Y-Mac, Young Men's Athletic Club or something like that. But everyone called it Scotty's, or just 'the tubs'

so life isnt always a bowl of shit. Sometimes you find I dunno, something that isnt shit, maybe it's just a rock. Scotty had a stable of boys, I think he rented them out sometimes, I'm pretty sure he did, I made friends with a couple, I knew they were turning tricks, but I wasnt sure if Scotty was sending them out or if they were freelancing, one day he asked me if I wanted to work for him, I told him I didnt need a pimp, he looked insulted, he said no, he needed guys to help run the club. He called it a club. He needed guys to wash the towels and the sheets, to mop the floors and wipe down the walls, take out the trash, refill the empty things, empty the full ones, whatever needed doing, and it turns out there's a lot of housekeeping to make a place like that work—you learn to recognize the smells real fast, grass is easy, poppers too, then there's that stale semen smell, and sweat, and sometimes shit and vomit, you cant expect the customers to clean up after themselves, they just come and go, we used a lot of bleach and detergent, so everything smelled like bleach every morning. Scotty wouldnt let us light candles, he was afraid of fire, the whole place would have flunked an inspection, it was an arsonist's wet dream, but we'd light incense when we could and that helped a little

Scotty didnt pay a lot, but you could sleep and shower there, so you made up for it by not having to pay rent somewhere else. And you didnt have to be out on the streets all the time, but you could if you wanted, because mostly Scotty's place was dead during daylight. You couldnt bring your johns back to the club though, you had to take them to the other place. Scotty had rules, he had standards. The boys wouldnt come back if there were trolls in the place.

I must have been there most of a year, I dont remember all the details, one day blurred into the next, but one day I realized how skinny I was, how many of the guys coming through were so much bigger than me, so I started going to the workout room. It wasnt much of a gym, but it was a good start, there were weights and pulleys and things, I think Scotty got them used from some other place that bellied up, but they were good enough for me. I'd get angry—I was always angry then, maybe I'm still always angry now and just dont know it anymore because I've gotten used to it, but back then, I was ferocious furious—so every time I got angry, and I couldnt stand it anymore, I'd go to the workout room and I'd do hurls, that's what I called them, other people called them curls, but the way I did them, I was hurling those handweights, those barbells, like—like I dunno—like I was going to punch out God if I met him face-to-face. And I wouldnt stop, couldnt stop, didnt stop until I'd collapse to the floor, gasping and hacking and coughing and thinking I was gonna die, and I'd still be angry, so I'd get back up and keep going. Half the time in there, working for Scotty, I was so sore and so stiff I moved like a zombie. In fact, that's what they called me behind my back, the zombie, I didnt care, why should I? I was the zombie, but after a while, maybe two or three weeks, maybe a couple months, I wasnt sore anymore, I'd get pumped up and I'd start getting that intense flush of feel-good every time I moved, I could feel it in my chest and my arms—the more I pumped, the more I could feel the rush.

and now I was hungry all the time, I mean really hungry. Shitburgers and fries werent going to do it anymore. I needed meat. Another couple months, I started getting hairy too, everywhere, I wasnt the zombie anymore, I was turning into a werewolf, well a cub anyway, but I could wear a T-shirt now and I'd get out on the street and I'd see guys checking out my chest as well as my package, it was interesting—no, more than that, it was exciting, it was a validation, I was somebody now, I wasnt just another skinny scowling brat, I was a proto-hunk. I raised my prices, yeah, I was still turning tricks, but now I was spending the money on chicken and steaks and fish, Scotty let me use the kitchen, I'd bring stuff back, sometimes me and the other boys, we'd all make a meal together in the private space, salad and spaghetti, sometimes a big meat loaf, more often we'd go up on the roof and barbecue burgers or chicken, a couple times we had ribs, and as soon as someone said something crude or nasty, I'd be off to the gym—it was a joke to them, but I could tell by the way they ran their hands across me when they walked by, I could tell they liked what they were feeling. The thing is, for the first time in my life, I was eating—and growing the way I hadnt ever had a chance to grow before.

I coulda stayed there forever—or at least until I got too old for the place, Scotty wanted twinkies and hunks only, you turn into a troll, goodbye Emory, that's how Scotty said it, I never found out who Emory was, but from the look on Scotty's face every time he said it, it must have been a pretty bad experience

like I said, I coulda stayed there forever, but I didnt. There was a guy named Peaches, I swear to god, Peaches, that was his nickname because he had this beautiful round bubble-butt covered with soft peach fuzz hair, his real name was John, but even after he said he didnt want to be called Peaches anymore, we still called him that anyway, the name was indelible. Peaches saved my life, not because he meant to, but just because he was Peaches.

see, Peaches was a regular, he was there almost every night, usually just before midnight, usually with some guy in tow, but not always, and he was a slut, and not just the coy kind of slut—he was the kind who has to tell you every detail how big, how long, cut or uncut, how deep, and all the positions, you couldnt shut him up, that made him a pig—inside and out. I suppose he showered a lot, he would have had to, but he just didnt look clean, you know what I mean? You've met people like that?

the first time I met Peaches, he was in the middle of a month-long exercise—yeah, I guess that's the polite way to say it. He was going to have a different man every night for a whole month, this was the third time he'd tried it, and it was the third time he'd caught the clap two weeks in, but he wasnt giving up. Scotty had a deal with Doctor Ellis—Doctor Ellis lived up in the hills somewhere, if you had a thing you went to Doctor Ellis, he was the only doctor a queerboy could go to, most of the other clinics wouldnt touch us, and the Free Clinic was another kind of self-righteousness, so Scotty sent boys to Doctor Ellis and Doctor Ellis sent back bottles of penicillin, Peaches must have been one of the busiest couriers, but it kept the fun and games going.

Peaches wanted me to be a notch on his penis too, but I just kept saying I had other plans. Didnt stop him though. Every time he saw me, he kept bragging he was going to get into my pants—I kept saying he'd never fit, I was still a size 28 and he was pushing 34 already, on his way to 36 and beyond. But he was insistent, he was going to bed me someday—I might have had my low points, but never that low, one day I turned to him and said, "You will never be that rich and I will never be that desperate." Yeah, that pissed him off, nobody ever said no to Peaches, at least that's what he bragged, so he announced to the immediate city—all the queers in earshot—he was going to read my beads, you know what that means? It means getting into someone's face and serving them a big cup of tea. Yeah, I see your confusion. No, not like tea the drink, but T the letter—it's slang for truth, you're giving them a big cup of truth, that's what you're laying on someone when you read them. Only in this case, when Peaches started in on me, it was a lot more like "doing the dozens," a string of nasty little shots, one after the other, intended to be so devastating my cock would shrink smaller than a virgin's clit and I'd just wilt away in embarrassment. He did it in front of everyone, a small crowd who loved to see him do his super-queer performance, and he went on about me, my looks, my behavior, my ancestry, my morals, my lack of fashion sense, my taste in shoes, you name it, he went on for several minutes—they werent good lines, but he was spewing them so fast he was showing off, demonstrating that he couldnt be stopped, except he finished up with, "You know about syphilis? Well, you're the Official West Coast Distributor!" He stopped to take a breath and I dont know where it came from, it just fell out of my mouth, "I'd rather have a disease than be one," and the crowd around him just fell apart howling. He looked at me stunned and marched away furious, and that was one of those moments when I learned I could bite back, really bite back hard.

only, Peaches went to Scotty and told him a bunch

of lies about me, and Scotty believed him and fired me the next day, he said he liked me but he didnt need the trouble, and besides Peaches was a source of big income and he couldnt afford to lose his business, so Goodbye Emory, he said it sadly this time, and he gave me an extra twenty as severance and told me if I ever needed help to call him—yeah, right, thanks a shitload, I'm never coming back here again, and that's how Peaches saved my life, I'll tell you the rest, what happened later on, a couple nights later, Scotty had a nice house up in the hills too, and he got into a fight with someone, I guess he had some silent partners in the club, I was never too sure about that part of the business, but Scotty got into a fight and the other guy got dead, Scotty got arrested, but he made bail almost immediately, and then two nights later, the Sheriff's department, working with the LAPD for a change, some kind of cooperation deal, went in and raided the club and that was the end of everything, and all those frat boys from UCLA and USC and all those little valley boys who'd come whispering through the dark, all those boys looking for a safe place to be queer, were suddenly being loaded naked into paddy wagons, clutching their clothes or trying to stumble into them, or simply still wrapped in their towels, and it was late enough, I heard Peaches got arrested too, so there was some karmic justice in that—I dont know what happened, if they were charged with anything, or if they had to call their mommies and daddies to get bailed out, I'm sure there were a lot of tense conversations in a lot of homes after that, but maybe some honesty too. Me, I was just glad I wasnt there. I knew my mom wouldnt have bailed me out. Once she'd given me my Christmas kiss, she was through for the year

but I'd moved myself out to the valley anyway, maybe I was hoping to find Joe again, but even if not there was a higher class of clientele. I went to a place

I'd heard about, called the Corral Club, another bath house, a little more rugged, a western mystique, like all the places out Cahuenga and out through Ventura had a western theme, the Hayloft, the Apache, you name it, but the Corral Club was right next to a recording studio, so it was ironically nice and quiet, I applied for a job there, told them I'd worked for Scotty, they pulled up their noses, but one of the guys looked me up and down and handed me a business card and told me to go see Mr. Foster, he didnt say why or what, I didnt have anything else to do, so I did.

Mr. Foster had a place in Van Nuys, Fulton and Vanowen, one of those cross streets, I think. I could find it again if I went looking for it. I didnt know it till I walked in but this particular boulevard was the heart of the southern California porn industry, which meant they had access to some of the best equipment anywhere, whatever wasnt on rental to whatever big shoot that needed the stuff, and not just Paramount or Warner's or Universal, but all the indies too—so all these old warehouses, I dont know what they were originally, had now been turned into studios

the buildings were all nothing on the outside, you didn't know what they were until you walked into one. The one I entered had a tiny little lobby and even though I might have thought I was pretty well-educated by then, it still startled me to walk into a room plastered with black-and-white glossies and color magazines and all kinds of posters, not just the walls, the ceilings too, they must have had their own print shop and if they didnt have their own developing lab, they must have had a pretty good deal with someone who could get flesh-toned inks and dyes at a discount, because that was the only color that greeted me when I walked in. I saw more pussies in that first moment than I'd ever seen before anywhere. For a queerboy, pussies can be pretty scary, especially if you're not expecting four whole walls of them—and the ceiling too.

The receptionist must have seen my reaction before, all wide-eyed and terrified, probably everyone who entered the lobby for the first time went all pussy-dazed, but she just smiled and said to wait, Mr. Foster would be with me shortly, so I sat on a couch facing a wall of pink and hair, and tried not to look like I was looking, I admit I was curious, who wouldnt be? All those women posturing, spreading themselves wide, sometimes with their hands pulling open the mysteries inside. For the first time in my grownup life, this little queerboy was, no other word for it, stunned immobile. I cant begin to tell you what thoughts I had whirling around inside me, but the weirdest one of all was that I was looking at where I'd come from, where everybody had come from, we all started inside one of those, we all came out of one of those, and that's when I just had to stop believing in any kind of god because that looked to me like the single worst piece of creation anyone could have imagined, this did not look to me like intelligent or any other kind of design. But then again, I'm a queerboy, what do I know about pussies?

"Eventually, about the time I'd passed from shock to horror, from revulsion finally to eye-rolling boredom, this guy Mr. Foster, he finally came out, I didnt know what to expect, but he wasnt it, he looked so ordinary, like the guy stacking cantaloupes at the Safeway, with glasses and a thinning hairline and a bunch of pens in his shirt pocket, and a handshake like an impatient businessman, which I guess he was. He walked me into the darker part of the building, except it wasnt so dark—it was filled with lights and cameras and three-walled sets, a bed in the middle of some, unless it was some other kind of fantasy, a dungeon or a desert island, slings and hammocks and things I cant even begin to describe, which is probably hard for you to believe, but even I have limits, and that was before they started inventing things with micro-chips and sensors and lubricants and weird new materials and high-resolution software to make it all work together just for a few minutes of escape to wherever it is you think you're going to—you want to know what I think, and I say this as someone who spent a lot of time in bed, on my back, on top, on bottom, upside, downside, catching, pitching, receiving, giving, taking, all the different euphemisms for pistoning one way or the other, and it's like I said to you before, I'll say it again, this time even clearer—most people, they fuck selfish—so selfish, they're not human. They dont fuck to connect, they fuck to escape. They fuck for themselves, not for the one they're with. They dont care if the other person has a good time or not. They just grunt and roll off and lie there staring at the ceiling, not even wondering if it was good for you too. At least when you're getting paid for it, it doesnt matter, you're not wasting your time, you're providing a healthy service, that's what they call it now—but what if it's a relationship, and it's supposed be that shit they call love? Then what?

so, yeah, all those stupid sex toys, you look at them—they're all prosthetics of one kind or another and they're all about selfishness, because when you're in bed with the thing, you're in bed with the thing, not the person—this little bit of happiness is for me, I got mine, and chuck you, farlie. The only thing I ever saw, the only one I ever thought might be unselfish, and I had to think about it for a long time—it was a two-headed dildo for lesbians, you could attach a little vibrating motor to it too, and I could imagine two dykes facing each other, sharing the penetration, looking into each other's eyes, and that was the only time I ever wanted to be a dyke, because that was something I would have done, because it wouldnt be about me, it'd be about her, watching her have a good time, but I never saw anything like that for the guys, it seemed the guys were all selfish pricks

but anyway, yeah—so Mr. Foster leads me past where they're getting ready to shoot, past these two bored-looking women and a guy trying to get it up, a fat fluffer on the floor in front of him, hardly anybody paying attention, leads me to an office where he sits behind a desk, sits me down opposite, there are stacks of film cans everywhere, and magazines too, some posters and stills on the wall, but not as many, Mr. Foster looks across at me and says, "You the queer, right?" I nod. He says, "Okay, take off your clothes, let me see what you got." He opens a drawer, pulls out a Polaroid and slaps a film-pack into it. "Let me see front, side, back—" It's a good thing I'd been working out, I've actually got physique. Mr. Foster snaps away, arms, chest, butt—the pictures slide out the front of the camera. Mr. Foster waves them around to dry without even looking at them, drops them on the desk. He takes a close-up of my cock too. "Not bad," he says. "How big is it hard?" He tilts his head, squints, trying to figure me out. "Top or bottom?" he asks. I say, "Whatever you need, I go both ways. I mean I'm versatile," then I add, "but I dont do pussy." He says, "That's all right, I already got plenty guys willing to fuck pussy, what I dont got is gay boys. You know what pays the best? Man on man. Because there aint a lot of guys, straight or bi or whatever, who'll do it with another guy. We got a few gay-for-pays, but they always look too serious, I'd rather hire a couple of honest queers who look like they're enjoying themselves. That sells better. You do three-ways? Leather? Any S&M? Maybe some bondage? Yes? No? We got a guy who wants a mummy film—wrap up a boy and the other guys at the party fuck him to death." He stops, he frowns. "Never mind, you're too pretty for that, you can be the twink, the college boy, the pizza delivery guy, the pool man, I know who to put you with." He scribbles something on a card. 'Here, go see Doctor Ellis, he'll make sure you're clean. As soon as he signs off, you call me and we'll schedule a shoot and see how it all goes down. You go down, right? Yeah, you said everything. Okay, get out of here, I got work to do."

Not the first time I see Doctor Ellis, Scotty sent me a few times, but this was the last time anybody ever saw him. A few days later, he got murdered. Allegedly by a couple of the boys who lived with him. Maybe not. I never heard if the case was solved. Was it connected to Scotty's arrest? Was there some other stuff going on that I didnt know about? Hell, yeah. There were always rumors about *those* guys, the ones who dont say much, they just show up and collect a fat envelope from time to time. But there was so much going on everywhere, nobody could know anything about who was doing what or for who. But yeah, that's how I became a porn star. For about three weeks. I made six videos, I never saw them though. My favorite was the one where this hot guy and I did it on the hood of a silver Corvette, I dont know where they got the Corvette, maybe it was Mr. Foster's, there was a dark blue background and a plastic moon with a light inside and some plastic trees behind, all kept deliberately out of focus, so it would look artsy, very artsy, like we were humping away in the moonlight on a cliff overlooking the beach below. He said he was straight, just doing it for the money, but he bottomed like a pro

yeah, that's the part I gotta tell you, Michael, all those big butch boys, its all an act, you get them on their backs, you get their legs up over your shoulders, you get their ankles behind your neck, and they just squeal like a happy schoolgirl who gives it up for the first piece of arm candy she can call a boyfriend

so I had a bike, not a big one, a little Yamaha two-stroke 750cc, big enough to look butch, if you dont know what butch is supposed to look like, but not really very big at all, but it was good enough to get around the city, faster than a car anyway, I bought it used from a guy heading off to New York, because he thought he was ready for the big city, I dunno what happened to him either

but it was my birthday and I knew my mother would have the semi-annual card and a check for me, it was her way of making sure I was still alive, and I was in the neighborhood, trying to see if I could find Joe's place, see if his car was there, maybe find out where he was living these days, but i couldn't find it, I'd never really seen it in the daytime, hadn't paid too much attention in the morning when we drove back, mostly trying to wake up, I'm not a morning person, hell, these days I'm not off life-support before noon, but anyway, I finally gave in to the inevitable, I'd been tooling around the streets of the valley for most of two hours, not having any luck, so I wheeled around and headed out to the apartment I'd lived in while waiting to move out, you want to notice, Michael, I didn't call it home, because it was never my home, only hers, the low-rent district of Van Nuys, everything west of the main drag, aging houses, shabby apartment buildings, and Sepulveda Boulevard, with its embarrassing string of cheap motels where you could rent a room by the hour, and an ever-changing selection of big-breasted women in tight mini-skirts just outside your door who'd be happy to spend some time with you for a small monetary endowment in return, you're not a cop, are you?

yeah, I went into the family business, my fucking mother, when she got desperate, which was most of the time, she turned her share of tricks, she thought I didn't know

she pretended to be happy to see me and I

pretended to be happy to see her too, and we made happy-happy noises at each other, until we were both too embarrassed to pretend any longer, she made coffee and brought out some stale doughnuts, she said she would have made a cake but she didnt know for sure if I was coming, and I said that's okay, I didnt know either if I could get away, and she had me there prisoner until she finally handed over the payment for my semi-annual attendance, and then I'd remember someplace I'd have to be and skedaddle out of there, straight to a check-cashing place

but this time, she went too far—no, that's not right, she always went too far, she always had to ask if I was still *that way* and yeah, I'd tell her yes, I'm still *that way* and it'd be like pressing a button and playing a tape, she'd say something like, "one day when you find a nice girl to settle down with"—and I'd usually bite my lip hard to keep from losing it, because what she's really saying is that she's disappointed, I'm not living up to her pictures, I'm not the son she wanted, not like my brother who's already off somewhere, Seattle, as far away from her as he can get, popping out babies, some of them with his wife, but me—I'm the runt, the failure, the embarrassment, and even though she'd never said it out loud, it was always there underneath, every time she said those words—*that way*—

and even though I was usually so good at not telling her how much it hurt to hear that shit, this time I didnt hold it in, couldnt, maybe because I hadn't found the white Cougar, maybe because I was just too tired to pretend anymore, and maybe because the whole thing had finally gotten to me, the war, the riots, the protests and demonstrations, all the hurting everywhere with no relief anywhere, but probably mostly because I was just feeling like a big prick, and I said, "Will you fucking get over it already? I am what I am—" and she looked at me like I'd slapped her, all shocked and hurt and victim-eyes, and said, "I just want what's best for you, honey. I'm your mother and I love you—"

"Yeah, I know. It's a dirty job, but somebody has to do it—"

And she reaches over, she puts her hand on mine and she does that whole performance of compassion. "Sweetheart, I just keep thinking that maybe if you'd met the right girl—" and before I could stop myself, I said, "I already did. He had blond hair, muscles, and a big fat dick. This long." I held my hands a foot apart. Okay, I exaggerated, it was only this long. Seven inches. But it was still nice.

She jerked back like I'd given her a fifty-thousand volt electric shock. She got up, she went to the junk drawer, how appropriate, and pulled out a couple of envelopes. "Here's your damn birthday card, that's all you came for, isn't it?" Oh, and the other one too.

I grabbed them both and headed for the door.

"Chase? Why do we always have to—" I didn't hear the end of the sentence, only the door slamming and I got on my motorcycle and rode three miles before I stopped and pulled the envelopes out of my jacket pocket, ripped open the card without reading it, dropped it on the road, so what, glanced at the check—only twenty bucks this time, cheap bitch—and was about to toss the other envelope when I saw the return address, the US Government, what the hell did they want with me

"Greetings—"

Oh fucking, shit, shit, shit, shit!

yeah, the draft notice, congratulations, you've just been given the opportunity to serve your country, travel to foreign lands, catch exotic diseases, and kill people

this is the stupid part—especially me—the war was somewhere else, it was somebody else's problem, not mine, I never took it seriously, because I didnt know shit, it was just like everything else I didnt pay any attention to, except now it was suddenly real and it was like this big hand reaching out of nowhere, grabbing me by the scruff of the neck and saying gotcha—

I show up for the physical, you gotta imagine all these naked guys, all my age, like maybe five or six hundred, all sizes, shapes, colors, big, small, short, tall, skinny, fat, stocky, you name it, a few real lookers too, except nobody's really looking, we're all walking around a little dazed with so much nakedness, not just our own, but everybody's, and the army doctors are processing us like so much meat, pee here, blood sample there, bend over

not the first time someone asked me to bend over, but the army did it like an assembly line, they had us line up, two rows opposite each other, turn around, bend over, spread your cheeks, crack a smile—the view would have been magnificent, except for the upside-down perspective—all those guys bent over, their legs spread wide, their cheeks held apart, revealing all those cute little pink puckers, a row of eager assholes, and the doctor walking up the line peering at each one, inspecting for god knows what, the johns on the street would have paid a fortune for the opportunity to pick the cutest ass this way—directly opposite me was another guy my age, bent over like me, cheeks spread like me, practically a mirror image, cute little red rose in the middle, just like me—we could have been butt buddies, and there's his face, upside-down, just like me, hanging between his spread legs, laughing at the view of my spread legs and puckered ass, laughing at my face, laughing at the sheer surreal absurdity of it, and me too, laughing right back at him, and I'm not the only one, all of us looking across the aisle at each other's assholes and faces, enjoying a moment of profound human silliness in the middle of industrial insanity and then there was the questionnaire, two or three or six pages, I dont remember—have you ever had this disease or that one, do you snore, do you have allergies, do you smoke, do you drink alcohol, are you addicted to any drugs, do you wet your bed, are you a homosexual? I marked them all yes, so they took me into a room, looked me up and down very skeptically, just like the johns on the street trying to decide how much they want to fuck me, and the one guy who might have been a shrink, I think he wants to fuck me hardest, he says, "Do you think you could kill a man?" I strike my best Bette Davis pose and say, "I'm pretty sure I could, but it might take all night." Ha ha, very funny, but no laugh from these pucker-faced men, they'd probably heard it before, probably a thousand times, and I must have pissed them off, because they passed me anyway

yeah, that's the hypocrisy, they didnt care, they didnt believe anything any of us said, I coulda come rolling into the room in a pink wheelchair with an insulin IV and a seeing-eye dog, they'd have still taken me

after we're all dressed, they line us up again, they tell us to raise our right hands, they tell us to repeat the oath, I mouth the words, then they tell us to take two steps forward to signify our acceptance, I'm tempted to step back instead, I think we all were tempted, none of us really wanted to be there, but maybe we did because there we were, and besides they'd made it clear what would happen if we didn't step forward, so we did, all at the same time, no, not quite, maybe I hesitated, but yeah, I did

you want to know something, Michael? I liked Basic Training, the whole thing, first Boot Camp, then Advanced Individual Training, it was the first honest discipline, the first real structure, I'd ever had in life, it was marvelous—the movies make it look like hell, with a drill instructor screaming in your face, calling you and your mama names, but everything he said about me was true, even more so about my mama, so all I could do was agree and congratulate him on the astuteness of his perception, but after everything else I'd been through Boot was easy, and AIT was even fun, because I didn't have to think, didn't have to worry where I was going to sleep, and never had to worry about what to wear, how I looked in it, or what message I might be putting out

but mostly it was because of the food, it was good and there was a lot of it, say what you will about the army, they fed us well—eggs, bacon, ham, sausage, pork chops, toast and jam, waffles and butter, pancakes and syrup, all kinds of potatoes, baked beans, grits, oatmeal, orange juice, grapefruit juice, tomato juice, coffee, milk, all kinds of fruit, bananas, apples, oranges, more food than I'd ever seen in one place at one time, and you could have as much as you could hold, and then they'd spend the rest of the morning running it off you until lunch, and then there was even more food, I pigged out on steaks and chicken and ham and mashed potatoes and gravy and corn and pie, and then came back at dinner time to do it all again, it was the first time in my life I had more food than I could finish

we drilled and trained and marched, we scrambled through obstacle courses, we learned how to make our bunks so tight a quarter would bounce, we shaved and showered every day—a hundred naked men all in one room and I barely looked at their dicks, I'd already seen my share of dicks, most of them standing up, so these were no big thing, we learned how to pack our ruck, we learned how to take a rifle apart and put it back together, we learned how to clean it and keep it clean, we put condoms over the ends of the barrels to keep the dirt from getting in, then we learned how to fire our rifles—oh yeah, and they hammered it into us, your rifle is your best friend, treat it better than your dick, there's a guy out there, his name is Charlie, he wants to kill you and make your mama cry, so your job is to kill him first and make his mama cry instead

we had a lot of target practice, a lot, then we scrambled over obstacle courses, crawled through dirt, and kept our faces buried deep in the mud when it was live-fire barely a foot overhead

we went out on bivouacs and learned how to dig foxholes and latrines and sleep buddy-buddy to keep warm, we marched twenty-miles in a day and came back shit-smelling and dirty, but feeling like we were accomplishing something, we marched and chanted and pretended we were hot stuff, and after two-three months, I began to harden up, I'd gained twenty-thirty pounds, almost all of it muscle, I saw myself in the mirror, I looked like the kind of hunk I'd want to go home with, and for the first time in my life I looked like everyone else, like every other man in the unit, clean-shaven, butch haircut, and an expression halfway between hard and naïve

yeah, I was surrounded by men, some of them even worth a second look, not that I would, I only look stupid, but I didn't mind enjoying the view when no one noticed I was looking, but I would no more have fucked my brothers than I would have fucked my sister, somewhere in there they hammered it into us that we had to have each other's backs, and yeah, if guys are shooting at you, that's a lot more important than having someone's backside—I'm sure it must have happened, some of those guys got awfully buddy-buddy, maybe they figured you're not queer if you're doing it with another straight guy—but that wasnt me

one day, they loaded us on an airplane and flew us to Hawaii, they gave us a meal, not bad, my first time eating pineapple, then they put us on another plane and flew us to some ugly dirt-red base in the warzone, all dust and barracks and shit, stinking of sweat and oil and more shit, and there isnt anything I can tell you that will give you a sense of what it was like over there, dont believe anything anyone says because it was all lies from day one until the last chopper skedaddled off the roof of the embassy, leaving behind all those little golden people who'd trusted us so much, yeah, it was ugly

that little sliver of country, under other circumstances, it might have been beautiful, maybe someday it'll be beautiful again, but when we were there, it was ugly—red-dirt ugly, red-dirt everywhere, like Alabama only not as classy, hot and stinking like nothing you can imagine—it was ugly from the moment we landed and stayed ugly until the day we left, except on the days it got uglier

but that wasnt the worst of it, no—the whole country stank of fear, everywhere you went, so you never went anywhere alone, you always went with buddies or you didnt go, and that was just the daytime—nighttime, fuck no, it wasnt safe, the one thing you could be sure of, as much as they pretended to love you, that's how much they hated you, that little shit-hole sliver of jungle had known nothing but war for ten thousand years, I'm not exaggerating, they were the Judea of Asia with one conquerer after the other marching through, we were just the current occupiers, so it was our turn to be hated

this is the point, Michael, this is the part you wanted to hear, I'm sorry I took so long getting here, but this part wouldn't make sense without me first telling you how I got there

most grunt units got pushed out into the field real quick, maybe the army figured that was the fastest way to get rid of the jokers, the assholes, and the ones too stupid to survive, I dunno, but we ended up in a battalion security unit for some of the bases around Saigon, so we had a lot of access to the city, too much maybe, we saw the worst of it, and even the best was a shithole

except for one moment, one place

I'm gonna tell you about Mama-san, the finest madam on the finest street of whores in all Saigon

except there was no street of whores, I'm making that up, if you needed a street of whores, by the time I got there the whole city was a street of whores, the whole country, that's what we did to them, we turned those beautiful little people into whores, all of them scrambling for Benjamins, but just as happy with Jacksons, Hamiltons, and Lincolns, if you werent choosy, you could buy a fuck for five bucks, boy or girl, as young as you wanted, ten would get you a clean one

but Mama-san had this house, it used to be in the French district, where the families of the French businessmen used to live, before they started fleeing the zone, and half the houses were abandoned, filled with squatters, the other half filled with various businesses, few of them legal, the Vietnamese were good at moving in, and Mama-san had gotten papers that showed she was the legal guardian of the property until the real owners returned, which was probably never, but it didn't matter, what she had was convenient, and her business was convenient for everybody, for the cops, for the military, for the locals, they called it the laundry district now, it was where you took your washing, or where you pretended to take your washing, but mostly it was the Benjamins and Jacksons and Hamiltons that were being laundered, how many of them were going north nobody knew

everybody called her Mama-san, if she had a real name, I didnt know it, and yeah, I know that "Mama-san" is a Japanese term, but not many of our boys did, not then, probably some pig-ignorant candidate for a body-bag called her that one day and the name stuck, so she was Mama-san from that moment on, everybody loved her because they wanted to believe she loved them back, but mostly she loved their money, at least that's what I thought at the time, but there was more to her than that, if you looked, but mostly you didnt look because you werent thinking about much of anything except your dick, Mama-san sat on the wide veranda, rocking and knitting, rocking and knitting, like someone's old grandma, nodding smiling with a mouthful of broken yellow teeth, what surprised me was the knitting, I didn't know that Asian women knitted, but she had this thing, I dont know if it was a sweater, a scarf, a tapestry, a circus tent, who knows, but it was all day-glo red and green with intertwined mazes of blue and white, very trippy, very psycho-delic, meaning you could lose your mind trying to trace the pattern—until that moment, I'd assumed that only old Jewish bubbies sat and knitted, like maybe it's a genetic thing, like cooking, and maybe women are born knowing that kind of stuff, anyway that's what I thought at the time, I didnt know better, I still dont, women were a mystery then, they're a bigger mystery now

Mama-san had four daughters of her own, and twelve daughters who weren't her own, sometimes she'd walk the streets of Saigon looking for lost girls, orphans, freelancers, whatever, if she thought they had promise she'd bring them back to her place, feed them, bathe them, then bathe them again better, teach them manners, train them—train them *good*—"Give soldier good time, happy time, he come back many time, bring friends. You steal, he beat you, he beat me, not come back, not bring friends. No steal. Keep clean, very clean—see doctor every week, take medicine, no sell medicine. Not keep clean, not stay here. No bargain, no cheat, everything fair. You know up-and-up? Soldier wants to have up-and-up and I not talking about just his cock. And now you listen good, most important rule—no drugs! You no use drugs or I sell you to cheapest pimp I know. We have booze, all kinds, we have cigarettes, we have Cuban cigars, we have grass, we have poppers, we have cocaine, we even have horse for special customers—but all that shit is for customers, you no use, you no become addict! Addict can't be trusted. Addict love drug more than Mama. So you choose. Mama or street. You keep clean, you hear—if you no keep clean, I no keep you. And one more rule, important rule, you tell Mama about every customer. If customer is junkie, if customer is rude, if customer smell bad, if customer beat you, if customer want special service any kind, you tell Mama. Mama has notebook, Mama keeps notes. Mama take care everything, you trust Mama, or you go back to street. You want street? Nobody want street. You follow rules then, Hokie-dokie? You be good to Mama, Mama be good to you."

the funny thing—Mama-san could speak three languages fluently. She only put on that stupid pidgin for the customers who expected it, the arrogant know-nothings who thought that Vietnam was their private whore-house and turned it into one—never noticing they were destroying one of the most beautiful places on the planet. Hot, muggy, damp like the inside of a steambath, but amazingly beautiful anyway, if it hadnt been for the goddamn war, I'd still be there, still wrapped in the arms of one of Mama-san's beautiful girls. Or boys. Yeah, eventually, Mama-san had two or three boys working too, Mama pretended they were tending the garden or washing the towels or repairing the roof, but they were too pretty for that—and the giveaway was when I passed an open door and saw Phuoc, who everybody called Phuck, the so-called gardener, all tight and wiry with muscles like taut cables, wearing only lacey silk panties, standing over the bed where Colonel Whatsisname was lying face down, ass-up, waiting for Phuck to live up to his name, I remember because he was just about to tug those panties down past the largest erection I'd ever seen on a Vietnamese man, if I hadn't already been in tow behind one of the daughters, I'd have been tempted, but Phuck wasn't there the next time I visited, so I missed my chance, someone gutted Phuck one night and left his body in the middle of the street as a warning—not sure what the warning was though—nobody knew if Phuck was killed for sleeping with the enemy or spying for the other enemy, too many enemies, not enough time to phuck them all, but we were trying to phuck everyone and everything, we believed we were up to it, because we were the biggest dicks in town, thats what Mama-san said and we believed her because we wanted to believe her

one night some pimp got angry, I heard this later, came storming up to Mama's house, blaming her for stealing his best girl, thirteen or fourteen years old, he'd just turned her out, Mama had a bad opinion of pimps, would refer to them with a stream of Vietnamese invective that defied translation, like a verbal machine gun, you wouldn't want to get caught in the spray—anyway, later on the pimp was found with a knitting needle thrust through his left eye, but Mama-san had a great alibi, over a dozen of the finest whores in Saigon were willing to swear up and down that Mama-san had been upstairs entertaining an important Colonel, assuring him that all her girls were clean, and could he arrange a few more boxes of antibiotics to make sure they stayed that way? Nobody was going to question the Colonel and even if they had, he wasn't going to admit how he was being phucked, or by whom, and who was going to risk his annoyance by asking him where he was on the night of so-and-so, they couldn't afford to have the laundry district declared off-limits and have all those horny soldiers do their own washing, either by hand or by each other's hands, besides the local gendarmes didn't like that pimp much anyway, he wasn't respectful enough, and by respect they meant he wasn't very enthusiastic about paying for their protection services, not on a regular basis, so they let the case evaporate after pretending to investigate, and meanwhile the point was made, you dont mess around with Mama-san if you like your left eye, but maybe that's why Phuck got phucked, some kind of retribution, not a good idea to pick a fight with Mama-san, she had friends, so if the body count went up a tick it was part of the price of business in the laundry district

but my first visit, my buddies, Perry and Claymore and Jake—not real buddies, not yet, but if you went out, you went out with a group, and they were your buddies for the night whether they were your buddies or not—there were four of us, counting me, I was invited because I had Jeep duty, an informal thing, but kinda necessary, every night starting ten-thirty, eleven, cruise the districts and pick up soldiers too drunk to walk, pile them in the back and drive them back to base, guys doing Jeep duty got well taken care of

so we arrive at Mama-san's, I'm still looking like a nineteen year old virgin, and in a way I am, still never been with a woman, only imitations, and I admit it, to myself anyway, I'm scared, do I really want to stick my dick into one of those things? But this is what makes Mama-san special, she's not running a whore house, she's running a "Happy House"—her words. "I no do whores. Whores dirty. Whores cheap. Whores have no self-respect. I have courtesans. Their job, give you happy time. Worth every dollah."

That was the giveaway. "Courtesans?" I said.

"Courtesans."

She winked at me and dropped the slanguage. She lowered her voice and said conspiratorially, "You won't give me away, will you? I do have a reputation to maintain for my clientele."

Later I learned that Mama-san wasn't full-blooded, she was one-quarter French, or maybe Dutch, her story varied depending on the listener, she'd learned knitting from her grandmother, not a lot of demand for knit garments in the Nam, unless you're from the Hmong area where it does get cold once in a while, but down here the weather didnt really encourage knitting, the only yarn was a silk cable suitable for fish nets and maybe parachute cords, but yeah, there's some crocheting and lace-making too, and it turned out there was some knit-work anyway because labor is cheap, and when you're on the other side of the planet, far enough away that you dont have to care, a bargain is a bargain, even a bloodstained one.

that first night, Mama looked at me and squinted perceptively, "Ghost-boy, you come in, come in— this your first time, yes? Mama knows, you need something special, ghost-boy, very special, you have Mama's special night, no argue with Mama or I throw you out, okay?"

I dont know if she spotted me as a virgin or as a practicing—practice makes permanent—homo, but one look, I could see she knew her business, better than I ever had, she had decades more experience. She looked at the sky, a dark low ceiling of gloom, "Monsoon, yes. No worry. You stay all night, special night for you. Phuoc take your jeep, wrap it nice, keep it dry till morning, now you come in, come in, alla you take off shoes, you have tea or wine, maybe beer, you start with happy foot massage, then flower-bath and neck massage, take alla war out of your shoulders, whole body too, and when you are empty cup ready to be filled, then you have happy night,

Mama promise, Mama knows best."

Mama-san didn't sell sex, that was for whore houses, if you were stupid enough to call Mama a madam or even call her place a brothel, she'd throw you out, cursing you with a fire-hose of Vietnamese, swatting you with whatever she had to hand, usually a cane but sometimes worse, she didn't hit very hard, but the invective was blood-curdling, I was never a target but I knew a couple of guys who regretted their thoughtless words, and heaven help you if Mama thought you had treated any of her girls badly, suddenly there were two strong guys in black who would escort you out the door very quickly, no questions asked, and it was not a good idea to argue with them, there's a story about them—that a couple of very mysterious fellows, maybe black ops, they had that look, they came back very politely, that is after they got out of the hospital, and asked if Mama's boys could teach them what they'd done, but Mama shook her head and said no, "this is a Happy House, no fighting here"—but maybe that's just a story

but yeah, Mama ran a "Happy House," her term, never any of those other words, I heard later on that some other places tried to claim that they were Happy Houses too, but nobody really believed them, Mama invented it and nobody ever came close to matching her trade, Mama actually liked making people happy, sometimes Mama would brew tea in her parlor and serve it to the boys, and sometimes they'd just sit and talk—or cry—I know because I was one of the criers, there was only one rule, whatever you heard in Mama's parlor, you left it behind, it wasn't yours to share, and if you broke your word and shared it anyway, you'd never be allowed back, that was the kind of power she held, but Mama knew what she was doing, this was her sanctuary and if she made it a safe place for her boys, then her boys would make it a safe place for her, and yes, she said, putting her hand on my knee and whispering in flawless English, dont you worry about Phuoc, the people who hurt him will never hurt anyone again, that was all she said, I never heard anything about any more bodies found with knitting needles in their eyes, maybe a chopstick but that wasn't unusual, but Mama had friends and that meant Phuoc had friends, so you figure it out, ghost-boy

that was what they called us, ghost-boys, not dead yet, but soon

I know, you're impatient. You want to know what *happened.* I'm getting there.

Mama promised me a special night and made me wait in the foyer while she tended to the others, after a while a thin boy came to get me, barely shoulder high, he said his name was Kim, he was wiry, not skinny, but neither could he afford to miss too many meals, he had shiny black hair cut like a bowl, like an early Beatle, I couldn't tell how old he was, maybe fourteen, maybe more, he wore someone else's pants that had been cut down for him, an oversized white shirt, a street urchin, wise beyond his years, unafraid, he took my hand knowingly, without a word he led me to a room upstairs, a room hung with yellow silks and vertical banners with crawly-spider letters, everything lit with red paper lanterns, he didn't speak, he moved about the room softly, making other arrangements as well, lighting incense, bringing out a tray of soaps and brushes, laying out a gold towel at the foot of the bed, until finally satisfied, he adjusted the lights, lowering them to the barest intimation of twilight, turning us both into sunset shadows

now he shrugged off his clothes, disappearing into his own silhouette, only the pale hint of a loincloth remained to give any detail to his shape, he was a dark spirit moving silently through the air he took me by the hand again, led me to a corner of the room with a tiled floor and a tub of hot perfumed water where he quietly undressed me, each heavy piece, boots and belt and pants, tunic and undershirt, all falling away like armor, leaving me vulnerable and naked, Kim had to notice me trembling, not in fear, not in anticipation, but with the strangely exhilarating experience of surrender to his patient and methodical attentions—I had done this to others, but had never been done to, never experienced myself as the client, Kim took each garment, carefully hanging or folding it, then placing it aside as if it were a priceless artifact, until at last, when I finally stepped out of my boxers, when I was completely naked and unashamed before him, then he turned his attention to me, looking up and down my body, fully and completely, first studying, admiring, meticulously tracing with his fingertips the outlines of my chest, my belly, and almost but not quite all the way down to

slowly and carefully he began to wash me, not quickly and not in great sweeping movements like an impatient teen, but like a lover, focusing his attention in measured precision, as if he was tracing the stations of the cross upon my body, step by methodical step, exploring my flesh, discovering the shape and feel of my personal landscape, a surveyor studying the terrain of possibility, and yet moving as dispassionately as if he were a groom tending a king's prize stallion—Kim turned me slowly where I stood, gently washing/scrubbing every part of me, my arms, my legs, my chest and back, my thighs, and yes, even the most private and sensitive parts of me, working unembarrassed, he made me feel noble, touching me first here, then there, turning me, lifting my arms, spreading my legs so he could scrub the places between, the soap running down my body, dripping and pooling on the tile floor, making shapes like glittering islands, I dont know how long I stood there, luxuriating as Kim slowly rejuvenated me, moving without urgency, as patient and as reverent as a monk, until I stood released and naked, unashamed and open in the night air

I had assumed when Kim started that eventually when I was clean enough, when I was ready, the eventual girl would arrive, but somewhere in the process, I'd forgotten about her, had passed beyond waiting, passed beyond impatience to another state of mind, a place in which there were no words, just a simple acceptance of sensation, as if I was already floating in the land of afterward even before we'd begun

at last, Kim pulled a stool from the wall, tapped me to sit, and began carefully and tenderly washing my hair, massaging my scalp and neck, kneading my shoulders, working his way down my back, never speaking, but always listening to the involuntary grunts or sighs I made, knuckling the spaces between my vertebrae, rubbing his thumbs and palms up through my shoulders as if forcing the tension up and out of my body, lifting my arms and rubbing the tension up and out through my forearms, my wrists, and even my fingers

and then the whole process all over again, this time rinsing me with perfumed water, yellow flower petals floated on the surface, everywhere that he had washed, now he returned and rinsed, spending even more time on the rinsing than on the original washing

at last, Kim held up a soft yellow towel, an invitation, he began patting me with it, stroking me lightly, barely touching, yet methodically making sure that every inch of me was dry, a process of physical affection that lasted much longer than it took to remove the last fragrant drops of flower-water, I stood naked in the dark, arms akimbo, no longer waiting, just existing, feeling ... something, I'm not sure what, a strange mix of sensation and emotion, gratitude/surrender/desire/connection, like a bell that had been too close to the explosion and was still ringing from the shocks, still vibrating hours later, the last remnants of sound audible only because the rest of the world had gone blessedly silent, that was me finally hearing my own self, resplendent in the calm

—something happened—

that was the first time and I didn't know what it was, I staggered, Kim steadied me, held me upright, studied my face, a question in his eyes, but still no words

and then the wind began and the pattering of rain and more lightning flashes too, and maybe what I'd felt hadn't been me at all, had only been the brutal crack and flash of thunder directly overhead, except maybe it wasn't, I couldn't tell, but whatever had happened, it had happened and I had felt it, and I wasn't the same anymore

Kim led me to the bed, pulled back the top sheet, and I lay down, first on my stomach, Kim straddled my back, once more massaging the tension out of my muscles, this time deeper than before, squeezing, pressing, holding, pushing, knuckling the vertebrae again, knuckling onto the small of my back, up my spine and into my shoulder blades, across my shoulders, again and again, I dont know how long it went on, an hour, maybe longer, until at last I felt so empty I could feel everything, even the slightest whisper of the breeze

outside, the wind howled and moaned, the rain hammered on the roof, the windows rattled in their frames, all the different musics of the night, punctuated with distant flashes and crashes, the drums of Asian gods, white-lit reminders of the red-lit war, violence on hold for a brief beautiful moment, the streets would be muddy by now, by morning most would be flooded and impassable, in my mind I imagined the worst, we could be stranded here for years

Kim worked his way down to my buttocks, my thighs, my calves, even down to the arches of my feet, worked his way back up, then down again, how many times I lost count

until it was time for me to roll over onto my back, as weak and as helpless as a naked baby, lost in the sheer physical joy of existence, Kim straddled me again, so light he almost wasn't there, floating above me, his only existence a pair of delicate hands gently massaging around my neck and throat, but with a strength that belied the fragility of his appearance, he dug into my flesh like a surgeon, he could have strangled me in that moment and I would have slipped away without a struggle, lost in the bliss of sensation, simply accepting the experience as the next moment of existence/nonexistence

but Kim wasn't planning to kill me, not that night anyway, his hands moved to my chest, my sternum, eventually my nipples—first one, then the other, I had not known until that moment how sensitive and tender a nipple could be, he pinched and rolled, almost but not quite enough to be painful, just enough to stimulate sensation, and then he lowered his mouth to first one and then the other, flicking with his tongue, sucking, stroking, circling the tip, around and around, abruptly nipping with his teeth to remind me of the dangerous thrill, balancing me on the knife-edge of awareness, focusing my attention on that single experience as if that was the sum-total of my body, my *self*, my existence in this strange black universe of death, emptiness before and after and all around as well but at the center, brightness!—I had not realized until that moment how intensely joyous a nipple could be, how close little Kim could bring me to fulfillment, my body starting to buck, gasps of astonishment coming from my throat

the storm raged around us, the house creaked and groaned, my body arched, my backbone knuckle-cracking as I stretched

Kim detached himself and floated above me, letting me ease back down into myself, he studied me with large dark eyes, I hadn't noticed until now how very large his eyes had become, how brightly they gleamed, how white his teeth as well, my eyes had finally adjusted to the night and I was seeing colors that could not possibly exist except at the very fringes of darkness, the enhanced awareness that comes with sublimation, isolation, and the resultant disintegration of all the hammering voices

"Hi," I said.

Barely a whisper, my voice still sounded loud, a rasp that scraped the silence.

Kim smiled back and finally spoke, his first words of the night. "Hello, beautiful ghost-boy, we make happy now, together, yes?"

he didn't wait for me to say yes, he began stroking my chest, occasionally brushing my nipples, reactivating them with sparks of blue lightning, but now his attention migrated southward, his hands stroking my belly, harder now than it had ever been before, but soft again under his delicate hands, too delicate for a boy, but that was the way of the Vietnamese, all so small and fragile-looking, but wiry and tough in ways we couldn't know, they'd had ten thousand years of war and occupation to boil the fat out of their lives

we were late-comers, opportunists, idealists, fools, thinking we were any different than all the others who thought they knew better than the people who lived here how the people who lived here should live, and just like all the others before us, we weren't here for the people—we were here for us and for all the things that greedy men wanted to take away from this land, so they sent us to kill for them—leaving behind little but vicious scars across the land, patterns of destruction, fallen bridges, burned out villages, all the evidence of our failures, bomb craters and the empty shells of barracks and bungalows, circular burns in the lush jungles where we'd dropped daisy-cutters to make hurried drop zones, scattered runways where death had been launched into the sky, and the rusting trash of all our abandoned machines, choppers and boats and Jeeps, and all the other little bits and pieces of what we assumed was civilization, Coke bottles and condoms, the steady devolution into garbage, land mines and waste everywhere

the little people looked up at us, the foolish giants, shook their heads in cynical amusement, hid their smiles and held out their hands for the Benjamins, the Jacksons, the Hamiltons, as long as you're here, we're happy to feed on your corpses, please lie down first

they could have, should have, slit our throats in our beds, but no, they were wise enough to let us kill each other, do it for them while they collected the pennies off our eyes, the blood on our hands was our own, they called us ghost-boys, we arrived already dead, the planes that delivered the walking dead were the same planes that carried home the ones who'd finally crawled into body bags

and in the middle of all this, the one truth that no one would admit, not even the ones who cried the loudest—was that this war was so much fucking fun, because we were super-gods wielding life and death across the land, from the bright blue sky to the verdant green deltas, this was the greatest game of cops-and-robbers, cowboys-and-Indians, good guys versus bad guys, anyone had ever invented, we got to get out there and play with the big toys, the big bombs, the big warbirds, the big everything—with orange flames that scorched across the canopy of the jungle and mortars launching streaks of fire into the night, arcing terror down on unknown charlies, sometimes screaming charlies, sometimes burning charlies, sometimes running charlies flaming through the darkness—we were licensed to kill and kill we did, joyously blowing things up just for the fun of blowing things up, bridges and villages, sometimes even temples, networks of hidden tunnels, trucks and buses, anything that moved and everything that didn't, boom, blast, boom, the more we loved it, the more they hated us, we didn't care

but in that night, that strangely silent moment in the heart of the storm, when Kim's eyes flashed at mine, the moment he became the boy-girl, the moment when I knew we were going all the way, fear and terror, desire and recognition, sudden awareness that we really were going there, over the cliff and into the abyss

—something happened—

that night, that was the night it began, Michael, I'd been in my own cocoon for so long I'd thought the cocoon itself was life, all there was to it, yet at the same time I'd been struggling to get free, never knowing what it was I was struggling against, but that night was the night I finally burst out, not crawling like an insect, but bursting like an explosion lighting up the time-blackened ceiling of the sky, shattering it with brightness, shards of light hurtling out and away, and here I am naked in myself, marveling at my own internal vision, indescribably something, maybe like a hybrid mutant cross between two impossible species, maybe an astonishingly azure monarch butterfly and a crystalline vampire bat, beautiful and deadly, and momentarily awake, still blinking in the first confusion of light and awareness, waiting for its wings to fill and stretch and dry

—something happened—

amazed at Kim's skill, the delicacy of his technique, the prowess of such a wiry little boy, even a little jealous—yeah, I'd read some porn, I'd heard of all those magical eastern karezza things where the whole experience was a mystical state that went on for hours and translated your being outward to a whole new plane of existence, I'd thought it was wishful thinking, the kind of erotic fantasy that teased with promises of nirvana—except the kind of people who were that obsessed with sex were the people least likely to achieve it, so wrapped up in their own impatience

but yes, I was jealous, no, not jealous, not that, but aware in a professional sense that there was something happening here that I'd never known was possible, I hadn't worked the street in years, would never work the street again, would never go back, but here in this moment, naked in the night, suddenly aware that there was more than I had ever known, if I had known such ministrations, I wouldn't have been on the street at all, I wouldn't have been that kind of person—and becoming even more aware that such abilities would have been wasted in that world, my customers didn't want intimacy, didn't know it was possible, the johns on the street didn't weren't looking for nirvana any more than a starving mongrel looks for filet mignon

and in that moment as *something happened* again and again and again and kept on *happening*, I realized that I had been one of those starving mongrels too

somewhere inside the swirling mass that used to be myself, the sissy, the whore, the porn-star, the draftee, the soldier, the ghost-boy, the whatever, that part of the self that still remembered the past churned in confusion, as if I'd been exploded into fragments, all flying apart like pieces, each piece a question, each a separate stabbing instance of existence, pain and pleasure and even worse, a terrifying awareness of all the empty places that had never come into being, a sudden vision that carried with it a horrible question, is this what it's all supposed to be?

and as it kept on happening, as the monsoon rains hammered on the roof, as the wind shook the walls and rattled the windows, as the night air chilled my skin, pulling me back into the sensations of myself and my body and what was happening

I knew what should happen next, I'd done it myself enough times, it was routine, not for everyone, mostly the older johns, the ones who'd already exhausted themselves battering against the brick walls of life, they sagged exhausted, grateful to be naked on their backs, like a baby waiting to have the diaper pulled off and mama or gramma exclaim in surprise and delight, "oh isn't that the cutest little thing" like they've never seen one before, and they drop another diaper over it so they dont have to dodge the inevitable fountain of joy, only this time the fountain of joy needs a lot more personal attention, so you straddle the customer, you play with his tits for a while, you let him get comfortable with your hands on his body, you can feel the moment when it happens, they lay down tense and insecure, uncertain—are you a good bitch or a bad bitch?—translation: am I going to get my money's worth?

so you start working them, kneading them like pasty white dough, they're all so soft, the hard ones dont need to buy it on the streets, and eventually the tension starts to evaporate, you can feel it, you learn the difference between just flesh and real muscle, you learn the intricacies of the body, all the penalties of time and abuse, but you never let them know you're noticing, and after a while you stop noticing, it's just someone to do and when they're finally ready, you slide your hands down the belly to the joystick, for some it's just a few quick yanks and they're happy, for others it's an all-night career, usually with a lot of mouth service, some boys complained about that kind of effort but that's what the customer is paying for, if you're taking his money you dont get to complain, I never did, I never minded, I found all bodies interesting, only a few were truly beautiful, but the most interesting were those that had been well-lived in

there's this thing that men do, it's the locker room thing, it's called "compare and despair"—it's where you look at the other guy's body, not just his cock, and you measure yourself against what you see, and—like a reflex—you can't help yourself, it's automatic, you wish you had his body or that piece of it that caught your attention, some attribute—you wish you were taller, broader, tighter, lighter, darker, harder, younger, older, black, blonde, red, clear-skinned, pink, golden-glowing,—but especially better defined, better muscled, better anything whatever

except there were some guys, you could see it in the way they carried themselves, they didn't care, they didn't look, they didn't notice, it didn't matter—they were living inside the bodies they were born into, comfortable, satisfied

like the old story of the guy who picks up a hustler, he drops his pants to reveal an erection only two inches long, sticking out proudly like a little pink baby finger, and the hustler looks at little mini-me and says, "just who do you think you're going to satisfy with that thing?" and the john says happily, "Me!"

yeah, that kind of guy, your opinion is irrelevant, there's something about those guys, a kind of confidence, where did it come from, I wanted it, not the performance, but the real thing, I wanted to find the source of that, I was a terrible whore, I was too curious, I asked too many questions, I made the men uncomfortable

but yeah, back to me and Kim, I knew what was supposed to happen next, after a friendly fondle, after a few yanks, or even a few affectionate strokes, after the preparatory hand-job, what passes for foreplay in a monetary meet-and-greet, then there's supposed to be a bit of friendly sucking—if he's paid for it, that's usually extra, everything is extra, unless he's getting a penguin—and then after that part where you show you're not afraid of his great big cock, if he's a young guy it's your ankles over his shoulders, if he's older he knows better and it's his ankles over yours, and then it's go until you come

you want to know something, Michael, something about tops and bottoms? It's all bullshit, all of it, there are no tops, there's only the race to the bottom, it's all about the prostate gland, that little bastard, it just loves to be rubbed, it's like adding three more inches to the back of your cock, three really sensitive inches, except the only way to reach it is through the back door—all those guys telling you they'll never let another guy shove his cock up their ass, yeah those are the same guys buying butt plugs and anal beads and vibrators, yeah, and throwing their legs up in the air in dark rooms when they think no one's looking, they want that little bastard gland humming with joy, and yeah, it *is* like being a woman, finally being vulnerable, absolutely trusting the man on top of you, surrendering to him, relaxing to his touch, even welcoming it—the moment of surprise as he enters you, the growing amazement at how good it feels, the discovery of pleasure, a different kind of *pleasure*, the naked physical connection of having him inside, seeing his excitement, even joy, as he pushes past the sphincter, fascinated by the sensation of that tighter kind of squeeze on his shaft, and you're feeling his stiff cock pumping into you, again and again, a rising tide, an ecstatic plunging, a joyous hammering, and when that piston finally explodes, so do you, and it's the most incredible intense astonishing, oh god, oh god—so, yeah, all those guys pretending to be tops, I was there honey, I know what you did, I know what I did, so you can just stop posing, you might be a drill sergeant in daylight when the sun is shining but you're a drilled sergeant at night when the son is coming—pay attention, Michael, because the last seven inches of truth is this, the bigger they are the deeper I get

so yeah, that's what I expected next, I was on my back and Kim's hands moved southward, down my belly, tracing the hairline toward the forest, and I was long since relaxed and ready, but no

something else happened instead

Kim lifted himself, used his delicate fingers to take that most rigid part of me and point it upward, he slipped the tip inside so easily I barely felt the entrance, and then slid down into position with a gentle sigh of contentment

the light so faint, I was seeing colors impossible in daylight, palescent and ethereal, his skin glowing silver-golden in the night, this naked boy straddled me like an Indian brave, bareback on his pony, riding triumphant into sensuous glory

I reached out and up, put my hands on his sides, slid down to his hips, his legs, and finally his thighs, his skin so smooth, as smooth as a baby's, as he slid back and forth on top of me, I stroked his inner thighs and inward, reaching for his

that wasn't there

my fingers slid and slipped and probed and abruptly—a wave of feeling, emotion and sensation, flooding outward from the center, a perverse thrill of startlement and discovery, excitement and amazement

—something happened—

for the second time in my life I was inside a woman, the first time had been two decades previous and I didn't remember the details, didn't want to

Kim's eyes were closed, she was somewhere else, even in the dark. I could see her smiling, it was all right, I wanted her to be happy, I wanted her to glow

and just that fast, both our roles were reversed, fragmented, reinvented, he'd been the whore servicing the john, now she was the customer and I was the service, I was someone I'd never been before, a man with a woman, watching her enjoy my body, so different than the way so many men had used me

it wasn't safe to be a girl in Saigon, so you cut your hair short, you dress as a boy, and if you dont have to bind your breasts, even better, and most of them didn't have to, you pass because you can, and those big stupid Americans can't tell the difference between one and the other, so you're a lot safer—mostly—if they think you're a boy, because they're all pretending so hard to be men when they're really just little boys with big dicks and bigger guns, I knew that before we got on the plane

I was fascinated, more intrigued than excited, how did this strange new form of sexuality work, I was coupling with a species alien to me, and yet at the same time familiar, like coming home, a process so natural and complete, it was as if I was discovering that all the laws of physics as I had comfortably known them were completely and totally wrong, as if my entire universe of physical experience had suddenly turned upside-out and inside-down

I was fucking a girl! For the first time in my life! Like a cold thrill up my spine, I realized I was finally truly actually losing my virginity, my penis was thrust deep inside a vagina—and even as that realization swept through me, Kim sighed deeply and pressed into me, and I arched my back, pumping upward and

—something happened—

afterward, floating in the land of afterward, that's what I called it, I dont know where I first heard the phrase, but it stuck with me—that moment of time, brief or prolonged, lying there, staring at the ceiling, waiting for my heartbeat to return to normal, waiting for the strength to return to my muscles, waiting for recovery, like a space capsule floating on the surface of a bright ocean of satisfaction, afterward I wondered who I was

suddenly aware that I'd been hungry all my life for a kind of sustenance that couldn't be found in others, it could only be created in myself and given freely, I'd been looking for it everywhere it wasn't—it wasn't the sex, it was the vulnerability, the surrender, the trust, the *connection*

Kim lay down on top of me, stretching his/her silky smooth body against mine, I stroked his back, her back, his pretty little bubble-butt, lost in admiration, was I with a boy or a girl, did it even matter, had I just fucked a strange little girl or a pretty boy with a pussy? How did Kim experience herself/himself? The way he walked, moved, held himself, he still felt like a boy, but she didn't

I wrapped my arms around him, holding her close, trying to figure them out, feeling grateful, amazed, complete, and wonderful as in *full of wonder*—this was the real shock and awe

we fell asleep that way

and stayed that way all night long

the first hints of morning, pink sunlight filtered sideways through pale white curtains, bars of horizontal luminance crossed the room, dust motes already sparkling, and a silken doll lay across my chest, she smelled like musky perfume, a suggestion of desire, I slipped out from under her, naked to the bathroom down the hall, still erect, or erect again, nature's little practical joke, a full bladder in the morning and all you want to do is pee and it's happily standing at attention

came back to bed still at attention, slipped beneath the sheet, Kim's turn to slip away and return, somehow still smelling fresh, she slid in next to me, nestled herself into my left side, ending up with my arm around her shoulders she half-spooned against me, and my right arm in an easy embrace across her boyish chest, my hand slid across her belly, her skin so smooth it was like outlining the silken curves of a porcelain doll, tender and delicate, then upward to the forbidden territories of her breasts, too flat to be a girl's, and yet now that I knew he wasn't a boy, I traced them with tentative reverence, recognizing now why his nipples had seemed so large, and the hint of deeper fleshiness that revealed the truth

then downward again, circling down across her belly, and farther south to a territory both familiar and strange, the mound of Venus and the valley beyond, it felt so strange to me to be stroking that space between her legs and finding nothing there, only the absence of an expected shaft, and realizing how familiar I was with male anatomy and how little I knew of this new terrain

my fingers acted of their own volition, with their own familiar mindfulness, touching, stroking, probing, exploring, discovering

Kim opened her legs wide, I raised myself up on an elbow, I hunched myself around for a better view, this was nothing like the wall of horrors in Mr. Foster's lobby, this was

—something happened—

I rolled over on top of her, she was so small beneath my bulk, I had never felt big before, but now I was a monster, she raised her legs, knees apart to form a sacred space, an altar, an invitation

it wasn't desire, not even passion—maybe lust, I

dont know, I pounded into her, a primal being, she gasped and rocked with me, I felt huge, but she was strong, stronger than me, meeting me stroke for stroke, and everything happened so fast

—happened—

Later, I came downstairs, Mama-san met me at the bottom, I was already reaching for my wallet, but she pushed my hands down. "You no speak, you no tell, you no say anything at all to anyone, you just smile and shake head—that only price you pay for special night, understand? *Capiche? Comprendez vous?* Kim your secret now. Or you never come back again."

I nodded.

Mama served a big breakfast in the morning, fresh fruit, bacon, sausages, eggs, croissants, and all the previous night's guests were gathered around a huge table, still in their silk happy-kimonos, and most of them with their "happy girls" giggling at their sides, pushing strawberries and grapes and pieces of melon at them.

Perry and Claymore looked at me curiously when I joined them, probably because there was no happy-girl with me.

"Everything okay?" Perry asked.

"Oh, yeah," said Claymore. "Look at him. He's got the Wile E. Coyote look. The bomb just went off in his face. The love bomb."

"You finally lost your cherry, huh?" That was Jake.

"We all have to lose it sometime," said Perry.

"Better than your right hand, eh?" Claymore.

Ignored the banter, shoveled eggs onto my plate, and bacon, and sausages. I picked up one of those strange crescent-shaped rolls. I'd never seen biscuits like this before. I broke it in half, amazed at its lightness, and spread butter on it. I kept my head down and focused on my food.

Across the table from me, was a man I'd seen around the base, he wore a gold and red kimono, he had lines around his eyes, he looked weathered, experienced, he looked like an officer, Mama didn't recognize rank, everyone was welcome. He studied me perceptively. "Leave him alone," he said. A bit of command in his tone. An instant pause in the chatter. "Mama gave him a special night."

The table fell silent. Even the girls ducked their heads politely.

"Well, tell us all about it—" Perry began.

"He can't," said the man. "That's part of the deal."

Another pause. Then Claymore. "So how do you know about it—?"

"Yeah, how do you know?"

The man shook his head and bit into his toast. He nodded toward me and I nodded back. A shared secret. Someone else changed the subject then, but I noticed the sideways glances of renewed respect and curiosity. I had a secret, I knew something, I was one of the *specials*. A legendary moment.

On the drive back to base, Perry and Claymore and Jake barraged me with questions but I just shook my head. Even if I hadn't promised Mama, I still had a dozen reasons why I wouldn't/couldn't share what happened. Most of all, because it was mine. It wasn't for sharing.

two weekends later, the monsoons were still raging, but we braved the floods anyway, we came in dripping and were met by a gaggle of girls with towels, I looked for Mama, waited until the others had moved beyond the foyer, I asked if I could be with Kim, Mama just looked at me blankly, "no Kim here, no such girl, you come in now, yes?"

I didn't move. She glared at me. "But what about the—the special night?"

Mama frowned, unhappy. "No special night."

"But—"

She turned to me, almost angry. "You have special night when you need special night. You no need it anymore, ghost boy. You man now." And she turned and walked away. It would have been dangerous to say more.

I won't say I was a regular at Mama's, but I wasn't a stranger either. I always looked for Kim, but I never saw her anywhere, in fact I never saw her again, I never saw any other boys either, although I'm sure if I had told Mama I wanted a boy, I would have found one in my room, but—in that frozen moment, in that separate space, there was room to take my life out, hold it in my hands, hold it up to the light and examine it, look for secret meanings, and try to see the soul inside, I discovered, I'm not gay, I'm not straight either, not bi and not tri, not anything, just human, quietly desperate and alone in my head, not caring about the form or shape or position, not worrying about top or bottom, simply starving for that rare moment of completion, that brief bright flash of connection that tells me that I'm not the only hurting hungry thing in this universe, even if it's just a splash of illusion in the night

sometimes I fucked, mostly I didnt, because it wasnt Kim and I didn't want to be one of those men on Santa Monica Boulevard who pulled over to the curb to examine the meat on the corner, I knew better now, so mostly I sat in the parlor, wearing a silk kimono, drinking tea, sometimes wine or beer, just listening

sometimes Mama sat with us, making sure we were all right, and one damp night between storms, one quiet night at three o'clock in the morning when all the fucking was finished but nobody was ready yet to sleep, Mama explained everything in just a few surprisingly literate sentences. "The difference between war and hell—there are no innocents in hell. You boys, all you boys, you're the ones who hurt the most. The men who choose wars, and war is always a choice, they sit far away with manicured hands as soft and as pink as a virgin pussy, they think they are clean and noble and right as they put their ugly guns into the hands of children, they point you at each other and turn you loose to die screaming in the mud—or worse, you survive and you come out the other side with your soul twisted like barb wire, and they tell you to be a man and not admit how much it hurts, dont reveal anything, tell no one what you did—what you're so ashamed of doing and what was done to you to turn you into that kind of person—tell no one how your innocence was shredded. That is the greater crime, because the dead do not hurt, only the survivors. That's why they dont want you to share it—because if you share it, the next generation of young men will know what's waiting for them and they won't go.

"Listen, now. Listen to Mama. Here, in this place, for one moment, you have a chance to remember that you still have a soul—yes, you are living through hard times, but you do not have to become a hard person. If you live, if you get home again, and no, there is no guarantee that any of us will be here tomorrow, but if you get home, now you have a way to remember that even in the middle of the very worst, there is a bit of your very best. No, it is not enough, it can never be enough, but it is a beginning. I had the chance to leave, I had many chances, but I stayed because I thought I could do some good. This is why I sit with you, night after night, I have fallen in love with you poor stupid brave idiots, you great clumsy warriors, I wish you were the giants that you think you are, but I dont want you to stop being so young and innocent and hopeful. I dont want to see you turn into men who wear faces that hurt from the inside. Remember this if you get home, survival isn't enough, there's something more than survival.

It's each other. Not the suffering. The joy. You learn joy here, you keep it safe in your heart, you understand?"

we nodded, we pretended to understand, but we werent there to listen, we were there to fuck, but sometimes, sometimes we did listen

the monsoons ended, the heat returned, a heavy blanket of air so thick you could chew it—and we slogged out into it, we shuffled along red dirt trails from nowhere to nowhere, every place looking like every other, and once in a while we set up a little base camp in what we thought was a secure zone—only later did we find out there was no such thing, the entire shitty country was even less secure than an unpinned diaper—and then we'd shamble out again, the living dead, already decomposing in the endless oppressive daze, a steaming ugly muggy green hell of endurance and

sweat, especially sweat, hot stinking sweat that rolled down my sides, dripped down my legs, soaked the corners of my shirts, left my underwear damp and chafing, made carrying anything an oppressive scrape, all of us slowed down, just pushing through the days like oil, we existed under water, the whole country was a steam bath, smelling of stale urine and fetid garbage, all of us crawling from day to day, each dawn the warning roar of another bright green oven—even those chopper-bladed fans hanging from the occasional ceiling did little but move the heat around

it was supposed to end, it didnt, it just went on, stretching into the blur of forever, we kept telling ourselves the weather was about to break, it never did, sometimes trails of white would roll across the sky, but those were mostly jet trails—when we did see clouds, they tantalized, but never offered relief of any kind, just more of that relentless heavy heat, day after day after day

and then one day, it wasnt
the sun wasnt a hammering presence, the sky wasnt an anvil of white-blue glare
we had fallen out of hell into a moment of fantasy
the air was bright and sweet, filled with cool breezes and even the smell of flowers,
we hadnt seen charlie in days, maybe weeks, maybe he had gone away, maybe our little base camp was forgotten by everyone, both sides
we looked at each other in wonder, we stripped off our shirts, our pants, stood naked in our shorts, reveling in the relief of a genuinely pleasant day
we laughed, we laughed at ourselves, just for being alive, still alive
for just that single moment of amazement, joyous, free, and honest, we were boys again, naked all the way down to our souls, for just that moment, free and unafraid
relaxing, we rigged up a shower, we shaved in our helmets, we brushed our teeth, we sat down to write letters home, we stretched out in the sun, enjoying our coffee for a change, we tossed a football back and forth, turned it into an easy scrimmage, tackling, sprawling naked in the mud, laughing at our rediscovered sensuality
that's when the shooting started, the boom-booms
the northern wall of jungle erupted, so did Jake's chest—a sudden splattering of noise, naked bodies twisting and bouncing, splashes of red—the rest of us dropped and scattered, scrambling in the dirt, sirens howled, men shouting everywhere, screaming, running for cover, finally returning fire, flashes beyond the barb wire, how had they gotten so close—
underwear, helmet, gun, and ammo, sprawling in a shallow trench, looking for a target, firing wildly in panic, then stopping, counting to three, counting to three again, catching my breath, feeling the crackle of the air, the ceiling of noise, bee stings of air, the

sudden thumping of the ground, things pounding down around, waves of dust rising, coughing and choking, gritty pieces pattering everywhere, fire flashing overhead, too low, too close

blinking in confusion, somehow I focused past the coils of wire, focused on the distant particles of orange flash, point and squeeze, leaning my weight forward to keep the gun from riding up, shooting in bursts, pausing not to have it overheat, refocusing, pick an area, pin it down, then move on to the next

and I caught the rhythm of the firefight, it's no different than the rhythm of a spectacular fuck, pound and pause, pound and pause, take your bearings, pound and pound and pound until you're exhausted and collapse—or cease to exist, which some of us do

but not all of us, we have a fire line and we're still pounding away at those little yellow whores, the same way we do at Mama-san's, pretending we're making love, not war—ha ha—all the circuits firing at once, the hammering in the heart, the frenzy in the head, another kind of orgasm, fuck you, fuck you, fuck you, all you little bastards

and then they come charging at us, through the tall unmowed grasses, red splashes, red bursts of fire and blood, shooting wildly, screaming

body parts shattered, jerked backward, flying away, an arm, a leg, a burst of flesh from the side, and somehow they still came at us anyway, staggering forward, shooting, shouting zombies—even after they were dead, they didn't fall down, fragmented horrors advancing across the mud and blood and red spattering dirt

there were so many of them, too many—we focused, we fired, we aimed we shot, we pounded, they floundered, they flailed—and one by one, finally they fell, and still they moved, crawling, scrabbling

spatter a burst of fire, pause, spatter another

burst, pause and spatter, splatter and—call for ammo, slap in a new magazine, and start again

and then suddenly, as abruptly as if a switch has been thrown, everything is silent and nothing is moving and we're all looking at each other in amazement and confusion, wondering who will be the first to raise his head, who will be the first to stand and look—is this another trap?

off to my right, someone stands and shreds the field with bullets, making sure

another stands and screams, spraying his own gunfire—in fear? anger? release?

others rise up to look in wonder, and finally, I struggle to my knees as well

my heart pounds in my ears, my shoulder still vibrates from the recoil of the gun, my mouth is dry, caked with dirt and blood, my eyes ache, all the physical sensations come flooding into awareness, a surge of being, my whole body trembles, my ears are roaring and I'm deaf from the noise, but I can hear the buzzing of the flies in the silent air, I'm fragmented myself, terrified and exhilarated at the same time, I'm still alive?

the first few men step ahead—tentatively, holding their rifles ready, I follow behind, still barefoot, the perfect target, wearing only a helmet and my mud-stained boxers, I hope it's only mud, picking my steps carefully, tracking potential targets, left and right, watching the world through my peripheral vision, hunter's eyes, if anything even thinks about moving, I'll shoot it—my hands tremble, reminding me to hold my gun tighter

someone shouts, points at a body, several bodies, the field is an abattoir, approach and stare, turning from body to the next

what kind of insane thinking—

who does this?

these men—staring dead at the sky, strangely

blank expressions—they had thin cords around their arms and legs, each with a stick tucked in, already twisted around, they came in with tourniquets already applied, prepared to be shot, but that wasnt the worst part, they still had needles in their arms and legs—those little morphine pops, you just jab them in, the bubbles already broken off, these poor stupid brave idiots couldn't have felt anything we threw at them

the sergeant bent, looked, touched, sniffed his fingers, tasted, spat—"yeah, they were so high, they didn't even know they were dead"

I had to stop looking, I didn't want to know, I didn't want to remember, but it was too late, dont be hard, Mama said, but how could I not? I wasn't the only one who vomited

and that was only the first day

after that day, it didn't matter what the weather was, we stayed armored up, we patrolled for real and listened to the night like it was full of enemies, because now we knew it was

every trail booby-trapped, mines and wires and punji sticks, ugly surprises everywhere, we lived in piss and shit and fear, days without relief, waiting for the boom-booms, waiting for the trees to explode around us

the daytime dance with terror, the nighttime sliced with bullets

red clay, red dirt, red mud, red blood, all the same now

it was months before the quiet returned, they said we'd won, they said we'd pushed the charlies back, way back, they said we'd broken their strength, they said we'd broken their tunnels, but on the ground where we lived, where we coughed up shit and dirt, we knew better—we knew we'd lost too much more than we'd won

it was more months before we were back in Saigon

again and despite our promises to Mama, we all had tombstones in our eyes just like everyone else who'd been here too long—just taking the next breath and getting to the next day was so important there was no time left even to think about fucking

but

one day, anyway

I grabbed a Jeep and drove into the city alone, not caring about the danger anymore, just desperate for something familiar, only everything was different now, dirtier, uglier, and too many uniforms on the streets, too many machine guns cradled in their arms, I headed for the laundry district—parts of it were rubble, burnt-out, but I found my way to Mama's house, I recognized the neighborhood, I found my way to where Mama's house had been—

broken fields and patches of forest, some carved out scars in the land, but nothing there, nothing to indicate there had ever been anything there, not even rubble, only a few hovels with patchy gardens, some naked children, an old man humbled over—I stopped him and asked, "Where is Mama-san? *Comprendez?*"

oh, he understood all right, he waved his stick at me and shouted, "Go away, ghost-boy, go!" I didn't get it at first until, face flushed with anger, he let it slip, "No Mama here, not for you, no more! Never! You go now!" Followed by a spatter of Vietnamese curses that suggested Mama gave lessons

back at base, a few days later, I looked for the man I'd seen, the one in the gold and red kimono, a quartermaster with a clipboard, moving supplies in and black body bags out, he gave me a curt nod

"What happened to Mama's?"

He didn't answer. He studied his papers, checking off numbers that matched the ones on a row of pallets.

"I went looking. Mama's is gone."

He stopped what he was doing and looked at me.

"You killed a man, didn't you?"

"I fired back. We all did. I dont know that I hit anyone."

"You did. And he died."

"How do you know?"

"Because you can't find your way back to Mama." He closed up his papers and turned away from me.

yeah, it was like that

who's the whore now, asshole?

two weeks later, I began using

I was a lifetime coming back, Michael, a lifetime.

—something happened—

and now here you are, like the smell lingering after a good fart, you come to me, all that uncertainty and fear wired up in your face, like that time adolescent you was inventing how to jerk off, like you're the first person ever to figure out how to feel nice, and suddenly it's exploding all over you and you look at the mess in your hand, not knowing what's happening, and you know that something happened, you just dont know what—and here you are again, another mess in your hand, still not knowing what's *happening*—and you want me to explain it to you?!

all I can tell you is that it's in my head too

all those lives

that arent me

but hurt just as much

except when they hurt more

fifteen o'clock

fifteen o'clock
light squeals in red and white flashes
I'm staring up into blazing noise—and as fast as that happens, I'm floating warm above the cold table, disassociating at the same time noticing in high-resolution detail, vivid colors, every thump and grind below, a body dissected by fingers of color, the spectrum beyond the retina, the lump of meat is filled with tubes

—and nothing happens—

black holes punctuate the white night sky, all lined out in neat rows and columns, I've never seen this sky before, but I know the lyrics, this sky this sky this sky's in love with you, floating alone in the whiteness

—more nothing happens—

a man, two men, a woman, I'm not sure, dressed in blue they blur, making noises with their cock-holes, serious sounds with many particles, syllables, I can hear you now, you know, they dont know, they dont notice, it's all numbers and machines, we have brain activity, dont get cocky kid, too soon to know, cant locate any family, I dont think he has one, I hate these cases

—nothing continues to happen—

comfortable in the land of nowhere, no feelings at all, I dont care and I dont have to care, nothing and no one and nowhere at all, the machines rattle and breathe, I drift and leave

—until something awful happens—

and I start to feel again, first a nibble, then an itching, a growing grinding, becoming a shrieking screaming, a roaring scraping raging burning—a hand on something that used to be a shoulder, and then I drift again

and existence continues like this in timeless forever, cycles of here and nowhere, until one day I'm awake enough to focus and one of the voices has a face and she's asking if I remember my name, if I know where I am, if I have anyone she can call, and a lot of other questions I dont have answers to, like can you feel anything?

she tells me not to worry, it's too soon, she pats my arm, I cant feel it, so she pats my chest, northeast of my heart, maybe she means to comfort me, the thump of her hand goes through me like a drumbeat, like I'm only a skin stretched tight across a giant copper kettle, booming at her command, she aspires to be Tchaikovsky pounding out the 1812

on the far wall, a horrible screen natters endlessly, splattering senseless pictures and grating sounds, I cant turn it off, it shows only blonde-haired women with serious faces selling grave lies and empty promises, they all wear red, why is that? I feel assaulted

no, I dont remember and I dont care that I dont remember, this is easier, this endless soak in cloudy nothingness, it's the drugs, I know, but nothing I recognize, never did the medicinal stuff, too clinical, too dry, too sterile and white, there's no adventure, no magic, I'm sinking, I know it, but I dont care, I float on the gentle tide of legal boredom

Michael comes to visit. Why Michael? I remember Michael—thirteen o'clock, we sat and shared emptiness in the night, I know all this without remembering any of it, I dont remember anything, but I know Michael, we could have fucked, he would have let me, somewhere inside he wanted to know what he still didnt know, but what he wanted and what I wanted, the two things didnt match so we didnt, and maybe I'm just too stupid to see what's in front of me, and why is he here anyway? He isnt even last night's trick. Michael talks, I cant, I have tubes in my mouth. He holds my hand, I cant feel it but somehow I know his hand is on top of mine. It doesnt matter what he's saying, it's all variations on the same thing. I'm sorry this happened to you, I'm so glad it didnt happen to me, so I'll pretend I care so I can feel good about what I'm really feeling, oh god you look awful, maybe you'll be lucky and die

nope, too mean to die, too ugly, the flying dogman fated to roam the black Earth forever, riding from one night to the next, hiding from the yellow fire burning the sky, creeping from the twilight of dawn back into whatever coffin I can find, escaping the heartless glare of day, only coming out again when darkness finally wraps a cloak of safety around the world, and there he is again, hunting the delusions of existence, the pretends of life

crowded into sweaty queerbars, looking for lust in all the long spaces, what's it all about anyway, the memories creeping back like worms—reminding me that there's identity, a name, existence, something that was *me*

but right now all that's left is *now*, a soapy daze floating on the surface, the murk beneath it still unknowable, just a cascade of words disconnected from reality, noises, all noises

Michael again. This time, the words assemble better. They say you're getting better. They're going to take the tube out. They say

who cares what they say?

white sky above, rows and columns of little black holes, blonde-filled screen hanging on the wall, promises and lies everywhere, Michael comes and goes, he talks at me as if he thinks I care, he comes and goes, and I see purple fronds, outlined in green, afterburned imagines floating on my retinas, the brightness howls, why is he here?

one day the woman in blue, pale blue, sits beside the bed and looks at me, actually looks at *me*. "How are you feeling? Okay? Blink twice for yes. Good. That's good. I'm going to take the tube out now. Are you ready?"

Blink blink.

"You might feel like gagging, try not to." She did something I couldnt see, then the rubber cock slipped out of my throat, I gasped in reflex, and she put an oxygen mask on my face. "Take deep breaths, but slowly. Dont try to talk yet. You're going to be fine. And yes, I know your throat hurts. It's going to be sore for a bit. Parched. We're giving you humidified oxygen. And in a little bit, we'll start giving you ice chips. I just want to make sure that you're getting enough oxygen first." She twisted around to look at her monitors, then back to me. "If you need to cough, it's okay. We want you to cough up phlegm. It tends to accumulate in intubated patients."

Heard the words, but concentrated on breathing. Coughed a few times, but not hard, so nothing came up. Not yet. Didnt have the strength yet to hock a loogie.

"Do you know why you're here?"

"Blink."

"Do you remember anything at all?"

Blink.

"That's all right. The brain is like a computer. The contents of the RAM didnt get written to the hard drive." Smile. "What I mean is, your short-term memory disappeared in the accident. That happens a lot. Dont worry about it—"

The accident?

it was the grenade, wasn't it—oh fuck man, fuck, it was the grenade, the goddamn grenade—it wasnt the first time I ever threw one of those motherfucking pineapples, I knew how to do it, and I totally fucked it anyway, didn't I—there was this convoy, when did Charlie get convoys? not a real one though, not like we would do, if it wasnt peasants on bicycles, it was beat up old trucks, one at a time, spaced apart so you couldnt take out the whole line at once, some of those junkers so old they needed walkers, and the first one almost caught us by surprise, coming up the road behind us, we heard it clattering up from half a klick away, it had a knock like a Brooklyn housewife demanding heat from the radiator

we dived into the ditch beside the road, a ditch full of dirty water, deep mud that stank of piss and shit and garbage, because every passing gook—yeah, we called 'em that, because we were the morally superior good guys, remember—every passing gook who had something to throw away or who needed to empty his bladder or his bowel just stepped to the side of the road and stood or squatted, not caring about the flies and heat and stink, this wasnt a country famous for its latrines, by the time we got there it was one big latrine, and there we were, ankle deep in stinking muck, crouching low in it so we wouldnt be seen and I was in the best position, I could see the truck coming around the curve

my plan—my idea—I was gonna run up just as it passed and throw a grenade into the back, they'd never know what hit 'em—except yeah, so I pulled the pin, took three steps forward, thought I was going up the slope, only slipped and skidded backward, arms and legs flailing and somehow face-planted into the ditch, the stinking muddy pissy shitty ditch, hands and arms squelching elbow-deep into the muck, I came up yelling, pulling my arms out of the shit and no grenade—oh fuck—you ever try to run in mud, it's like one of those bad dreams where you're trying to run and you're not moving, only this was for real—the fucking pineapple went off when I was only a few feet away, the pack on my back taking most of the blast, but still knocking me flat—back into the muck—nothing injured but my pride

picked up a new nickname that day too, not gonna share it here

no, no—that wasn't it—it wasnt the grenade, that was another time, long ago—when I still had both legs—but the memories are mixed up again because

all time is collapsed

—something happened—

I open my eyes and Michael is sitting beside my bed, I dont know why, what the fuck are you doing here

He shrugs, "Saw your picture in the news, told 'em I was your brother."

"Why?"

He shakes his head. "I dunno." Adds, "Maybe I think you're the only honest person I know."

had to stop and think about that

me, honest? how the fuck did that happen?

and then, the next thought—you really dont know me very well, do you?

and the one after that—jeez, you stupid fuck, what kind of a life are you living that you think I'm honest

"I care about you," he says—there it is—like a loaded gun pointed at my head, because now I'm supposed to say the same thing back at him, and I stopped caring about anything and anyone a long time ago, because I found out how much it hurts and I'm not going there anymore

caring? it's lo-fat love

and love is poisonous, it's toxic, and it's a lie that we tell ourselves—that we fall into it, like one of those hidden tiger traps with toxin-tipped punji sticks at the bottom—except we dont fall into it, we jump into it eagerly, we *choose* it—

we look at all the little pieces, the color of the eyes, the curve of the neck, the shape of the nose, the fullness of the lips, the clarity of the skin, the underlying bone structure, we decide this thing, this body, is attractive, we choose to find out who or what is living inside, and if there's even a hint of a smile, we pull out the list—the soul-mate list—and start checking off all the necessaries

we choose it, it doesnt just happen, we choose it, that's the terrible truth about caring, and all the things that follow after, so why me, Michael—why did you choose me?

and why the hell should I choose you?

all I did was tell you the truth

oh

okay, yeah—I guess that was honesty

if caring is a choice, then honesty's a drug—the worst one of all, because there's no cure for it, no rehab, you get one sniff of honesty, one little taste, you hunger for it the rest of your fucking life—you want to mainline it, you keep chasing it until you find the hard baked floor of truth at the bottom—or even more important, the lie it's built on

because once you find the lie at the bottom, you can disregard everything built on top of it, you can go back to your safe little prejudices

that's what you're coming back for, isnt it—the lie—you want to see me bottom out, the part that hurts so bad it isnt even words anymore, just a gut-twisting scream that scrapes the lungs and tears the throat with the force of its release—because if can you find that part of me, then you'll know I'm not what you think, never was—that'll be your revenge, not just for that first horrible shocking kiss, but for everything that followed after, the horrendous car-crash impact of discovering there's another way to think and be on this planet, something more than hiding in boxes

you dont really care, that's just the bullshit excuse—what you want is something darker and uglier, you think I dont know

I'll give you the short version—at the bottom, you'll find the shrieking piece within still demanding to know what the fuck just happened—that's the hypocrisy of the universe, the colossal practical joke of life, you think when you die, that's when you're going to get it all explained—fuck no, there is no explanation, it's all empty, it's all meaningless, and we're battering around in it like shining steel spheres in a pinball machine

if it's ever going to mean anything, it isnt—in three billion years, the sun still burns out, and the first thought in your head when you hear that is 'what's in it for me?'—and as soon as you figure out there's nothing in it for you, you stop thinking about it

there, that's the meaning of life

what's in it for me?

here's the clue

—nothing happened—

okay, Michael yeah, you can have it—I'll take it out of my head and put it into yours, and you carry it around for the rest of your life, not me

because I'm not gonna be here much longer and this pain is too good not to share

see

there's a time bomb in my head, ticking away so silently I have no idea when it will go off—maybe it will happen in my sleep and I will disappear quietly, more likely there will be a moment of sharp stabbing pain, or confusion, possibly even a flash of awareness—*this is it!*—there's no way to know

you think I know something?

I know nothing

the difference between you and me, Michael, is

that I know I know nothing

who am I, what am I, it doesnt matter anymore, I'm the place where all this shit happened, I'm the part of the universe that lived it, breathed it, smelled it, tasted it, and survived just long enough to know how much it all hurt, so yeah—that's who I am, that's the all of it

do I take off my plastic leg to fuck, is that what you want to know?—the answer is I dont know, because I dont fuck anymore, no one wants me—I'm old, ugly, scarred, and broken, mine isnt the face you want to see when you're coming—when I look into the abyss, the abyss flinches, fuck Nietzsche

—nothing happened—

there—that's the punch line, nothing, nothing, nothing happened

except just this little flicker of confusion

when I was a kid, your age, Michael—yeah, I know, you think you're a grownup, it says so on your driver's license, ha—I read Burroughs and Kerouac, Ginsberg and Rechy and Vassi, I sat through movies like *Easy Rider* thinking, yeah—that's it, that's what freedom looks like, sex, drugs, and rock'n'roll—what bullshit, a fuckin lie, a mirage, a reflection of water on the edge of the road ahead, we chase it across the desert, never catching up because it was never there in the first place, an impossible illusion, a pretentious delusion, a mass confusion

I see guys still chasing it, still believing the lie, still getting on their bikes and searching for America, except America isnt there anymore, hasnt been there for half a century, not since we paved it over with the Eisenhower Memorial Autobahn—you get off anywhere, it's the same six plastic franchises and every place looks like every other place, so why go anywhere, the McFuck you buy in Missoula is going to taste exactly the same as the one you bought in Waco you want to see what's left of the place we used to believe in, the place that was never there no matter how hard we believed, you gotta get off the interstate and prowl the back roads, the abandoned places, the little towns that still scrabble for crumbs of existence, the places where people have a past and even remember a few last pieces of it

but even that's dying now—they got the internet feeding them facebooks and pirate bays, they got smart phones full of games and apps, they got wall-sized 3D satellite-powered TV with 500 channels, and they dont even have to walk out the front door to shoot the zombies, they're already zombified, the infection started eating their brains before their parents were born

people dont even know how to fuck right

oh, now I have your interest?—okay, I'll 'splain you, loosely

it's about porn

porn is how America teaches its children about sex, it's an idealized—no, what's the opposite of idealized, that's what it is—it's desperate frenzied grappling, it's humping and pumping and bumping, it's all about cocks and cocks and pussies and pussies, and did you ever look at the faces, theyre not having any fun, theyre impatient to get to the paycheck, because theyre not human beings, theyre whores—porn whores—people you pay so you can watch them fuck—and that's a bigger lie than "the check is in the mail" or "I wont come in your mouth"—because real sex is nothing like that

see, when I was a kid, porn was mostly pictures in magazines you hid under your mattress—and you had to use your imagination, wow gee, what will that be like when I finally get a chance to do it with a real boy or a real girl, I didnt care, I just wanted someone to want me as much as I wanted them, so for me, all that porn wasnt about who was doing what and with which and to whom, it was about how maybe two people could have fun together

it was a long time before I had that, I'll get there, but it's a long ugly journey

the point is—porn is now some kind of electronic assault, inescapable, it follows you everywhere, anywhere you have a screen, it pours in from the internet and it's one long lie, telling you everyone's beautiful and horny and can hardly wait, sex is everywhere—as soon as the pizza boy arrives, he's ready to drop his pants, he's not a human being, he's just a delivery system for cock, and the women—what porn tells you about women is so wrong, so ugly, so disgusting, you have to wonder if the guys behind the camera ever knew a real woman, let alone got into bed with her

because all that crap, streaming in—all those megabits per second—all that shit tells you that sex is a desperate grapple, a mad scramble for the money shot, and two shots later you switch partners and do it all again

and that's bullshit and anyone who believes that, who falls for that crap, he's not just an idiot, he's delusional

in real life—it's not like the movies where two people look at each other, grab each other, then suddenly they're sucking each other's brains out through their mouths—fuck, no—that's not kissing, that's hoovering—real kissing, c'mere, I'll show you—it's slow and easy and fun, not desperate, it's a dance, ballet, a *pas de deux*—you're surprised I know those things, I only look stupid, my life is more than you've imagined

I read a book—it was about Eskimos, I dont know if it was true or not, but the way the Eskimos in the book talked about sex, they didnt have a word for sex, they called it "laughing with"—he didnt fuck his wife, he laughed with her, I didn't understand that, not then anyway, maybe later, too much later

because porn teaches us that sex is a serious business, mostly a business, and I'd been in that business long enough to know that it uses people up and throws them away like a Kleenex full of come

we like fucking so much, we forget to make love

and even when we do remember, we still forget

still with me?

it gets worse

there's this guy named Kerouac and he writes this book, *On The Road*, about his adventures—but mostly it's about this guy Dean, except in real life his real name was Neal Cassady, and in the book he comes off as a charming asshole, a charismatic loser, a delicious scoundrel, but a sociopath of the purest kind, using people, using them up, leaving Kerouac almost dying of dysentery in Mexico, because he just didnt want to deal with it, and why would I want to read about an asshole like that or the asshole who kept enabling him—I guess it had to be the quality of the writing that kept me reading, because I just wanted to grab Dean and punch the shit out of him, almost from the first page he shows up, and if Kerouac was all that smart and insightful and perceptive, then why the fuck did he waste so much time on this guy, I wouldnt have—and that was the real question that I slammed up against, why the fuck was he worth reading about anyway—well, no he wasnt, what was worthwhile was Kerouac's journey, not his, but jeezis, why the fuck did he have to take the long way around?

but what the fuck, so many of us did the same thing on our own twisted roads, thinking that the beat, the jazz, the weed—that all that stuff was some kind of freedom, some great magical journey of discovery, here's the meaning of life and everything, meanwhile all you're really doing is living with hobos, picking crops with braceros, maybe getting laid off some blowsy waitress hungry for escape, all the while pretending you're the next John Steinbeck, but meanwhile stealing from the faded little mom-and-pop stores and gas stations along the way, just being arrogant and selfish everywhere, and thinking that's the adventure of life

fuck no, just fuck no

and all the other guys who came after them, writing the same kind of shit, Rechy and Vassi and all the rest—their adventures on the underside of life, as if writing a book about it somehow ennobles it, fuck no, shit is still shit, even if you're selling it hardcover

maybe they were fools and assholes, but the bigger fool was me, the bigger asshole, because I believed it, I believed all that crap was important, I believed it for way too long, and by the time I figured it out—it was too late, I'd already used up my chance

yeah, I know, you're getting impatient, where's the story man?—the explanation, the insight, the epiphany is supposed to go at the end, not the beginning, well that shit wasnt the epiphany, it's just the warmup, it's me telling you what a big bag of shit I was, because none of the rest of this makes any sense if you think I was anything else

there was me and there was the hog and there wasnt anything else, there wasnt no laughter, there wasnt no laughing with, there wasnt anything but the belch of fumes and a scowl and a growl to keep the rest of the world cowering at a distance, which they did real well, I sure showed them

that hog and me, we were like this thing coming out of the dusty horizon, you'd hear the rumble long before you saw anything, and then I'd ride in and I could see the women grabbing their curious children and hurrying them indoors, before the monster boogeyman swooped in and snatched them up and rode off with them, yeah—that was me, I never stayed any place long, by popular demand

I'd ride until I got tired of riding, until I came to someplace that I wanted to stop, usually someplace there werent too many people, they bothered me almost as much as I bothered them, but I knew some folks, I knew some places to go, places where I could hang for a bit, so I'd do some stuff, whatever needed doing, until it was time to move on again—aint too proud to wash dishes if I have to, but I can patch a tire, change your oil, tune an engine, take it apart and put it back together again better'n new—aint interested in doing much more than that, what they call a job, a career, that's a trap, ties you down, glues you to a place, same with family, only worse—there's no freedom to get on the bike and leave it all behind, easier to not have one

and after a while, all the places blur into the same place, and I keep riding, looking for a place that isnt the same, and eventually, I'm somewhere so far away from anywhere, I could be on another planet altogether, I'm not sure how many suns are in the sky, how many moons are whirling across the night

here's how fucked up I am, I'm in the middle of somewhere, not quite the end of the universe, but I think I can see it from here, a place where the sky is white all the time, and I'm learning the way of the whaqui, except I dont speak the language, *no habla human, no comprendo, gracias, por favor, etc.*

and then one night, so clear the stars cant twinkle, there's not enough air in the air, the madman pours me tea, and after a long long silence, he says to me, can you feel it?—where did the madman come from and how long have I been sitting here in the dark with him, I'm suddenly awake for the first time in how long?—and he asks, can you feel it, and I'm not sure what he's asking, I tell him I'm trying not to feel anything anymore, he says that day will come soon enough, why hurry it—

in the clear, stripped of all the jumbo-mumble, he says what's wrong with human beings—as soon as we discover that we can feel, we spend the rest of our lives trying not to—pills and drugs and the search for truth

as if understanding the universe will make it stop hurting?

yeah, I get it—you cant win, you cant break even, but yeah, you can get out of the game, is that what you want?

somewhere in that mumble, I get my own words out, I tell him about the

—something happened—

moments that happen in my life, I dont know what they are or why, and he nods knowingly, a smile of broken yellow teeth, surrounded by a face of wrinkles and eyes that sparkle like God, he says yes, you are feeling it—

but what am I feeling?

what he says makes no sense, he says it's unraveling, all of it, the threads are snapping and every time one snaps

—something happens—

and he just laughs and says yes, it's because we've forgotten how to be human, and I snap back that I never learned how, there was no one there to teach me

he laughs again, leans across and taps my chest with a bony finger—in there, in there, there was always someone there to teach you, in there

—in here? In here? are you fucking kidding me? in here is so fucked up, so twisted and ugly, it's nothing, it's not who I am, it's not who I want to be—

es correcto, that's right, he leans even closer—it is not who you want to be, but that's who you have chosen to be, because that's what you've been listening to

that's all there is

if you say so

are you saying there's more?

no sé, I dont know what is inside of you, only you can say—if there is more, you dont hear it because you're not listening for it, perhaps you have never listened to anyone else either, and that is the saddest thing of all, because that makes you the most alone thing you can be—he leans back again

and I stare at him, comprehending and not at the same time

and maybe that's when the drugs kick in, because all I see are his eyes and his voice is coming from someplace else, like outside of the world maybe

his words have colors and flavors and a bitter edge

you come from a place where no one listens and you think that's the world, then you come out here to this place where there is nothing and everything, all at the same time, you think this is a holy place, but it's no holier than any other place, except you want it to be—and you still cant listen because you only know how to listen to the noises of other men—and here you sit, baking like a lizard on a log, looking for reality by trying to escape it

you say you cant hear it—and when you speak it aloud, you make it real in the world—

eres una cucaracha, you are a cockroach at the feast of life, you cant hear what's happening precisely because you keep saying you cant hear what's happening

then teach me, I tell him, that's why I'm here

I already taught you, he laughs again, but you keep speaking from the past—the world you believe, not the world that can be—*idiota*, you have to pour the piss from your boot before you can read the instruction on the heel

I get angry, I get frustrated, I sip more tea and strange colors flash across the sky

if this asshole understands it, he cant explain it in

language I can understand, and

—something happens—

in the morning he's gone, I'm alone on the floor of the gritty desert, just me and the bike and the patient bright eye in the sky

if this is enlightenment, it doesnt work

I get on the bike, I ride, the world blurs behind me

how many sunsets, how many places, I dont know, I'm not counting, I'm just sliding through a landscape of joints and tequila, cactus and mushrooms, and strange crazy men who can hear colors and I dont know what color my submarine is anymore, someone tells me that my aura is black, except when it isnt, the crystal ship is leaving for another planet, but that's not a trip I want to take, I get on the bike again and ride back through the looking glass, except I've forgotten which side of it I'm on

until somewhere in Arizona, a two-lane road leftover from before the war before the war before the war, when crumbling old trucks, overloaded with beds and chairs and children, clattered west out of the dust bowl toward the illusions of California, you could still see the occasional rusting carcass, or maybe a couch, a stove, sometimes an old mattress, or a busted toilet, scattered along the side of the road

calling it a road is flattery, it's cracked and pitted and potholed, I'm riding slow, partly because the pavement is a jigsaw puzzle of broken pieces and partly just to enjoy the heat of the desert, when a coupla assholes in an orange GTO comes racing around me, slicing in front of me, on purpose, just so his passenger can yell—"faggot hippie!"—and I go skidding out of control, I only look stupid, I lay the bike down and slide sideways into a nice soft sand dune, scraping hell out of my leg—but it was the plastic one, so that hardly hurt at all, I can imagine the rednecks in the GTO laughing hysterically, they dont even slow down, theyre having beer and giggles, they aint coming back to see if I'm dead, I'm not, but I'm not happy either

but I can stand and that's usually enough, being able to stand, that's my mantra, "I'm still standing"—yeah, take your best shot, I've been through worse shit than this and I'm still standing, at least they weren't throwing mortar shells

got the bike perpendicular, not an easy thing, that hog was heavy and I didn't have the leverage I needed, but somehow, anyway, even though it left me red-faced and panting and sweating like a one-legged man who's just pushed 800 pounds of motorcycle upright, and that was the easy part, because goddammit, it wouldnt start and I had nothing but miles between me and the next bottle of beer, crap knows how far to a repair shop

so I start pushing that chunk of broken metal down that long burning highway, pushing through that sweltering blanket of Arizona heat, the only possible relief the near-freezing Arizona night, if I last that long, but right now, under the glaring white eye of the scorching desert sun there's nothing to do but lean on the handlebars and push, one step at a time, and even the plastic leg is starting to hurt, not just the stump, the whole imaginary leg, one foot in front of the other, like in the Delta, because to stop is to die, so just keep pushing, just keep pushing

maybe an hour, maybe two, maybe longer, I wasn't wearing a watch anymore, nobody stops to help anyway, they just go roaring by in their flashy m&m colored Detroit pig-iron, laughing, shouting obscenities, until I hear this rattling clanking noise behind me, and this battered old rust-red Chevy pickup slides to a halt a few lengths ahead of me and three longhair boys pour out, theyre wearing cut-offs and sandals and not much else, and if I hadnt been approaching death coming back from the far side, I'd have let myself imagine them undressing, except they were already mostly there, so I just straightened as best as I could, my back complaining like a single mom with a squalling kid and a drunken –ex

the first one, piles out of the driver side, sandy-haired and lean,
Arizona has baked the fat off him, he brings me a water bottle, one of those new plastic ones like they sell sodas in, the water's warm, but it's water and I'm so dry I stopped sweating ten miles back, nothing left to sweat, and my throat is so dry I can't even croak out a thank you, and even though I know better I just pour it all back and I admit, for a moment I'm so dizzy I think I'm going to fall over, but the other two boys are there to catch me and that wouldnt be so bad, there's something about them, and yeah, that's my first experience with the glow, even though I didn't recognize it then

the driver, the one who hands me the water, his name is Shine, not the name someone else gave him, just the name he chose, it's the way he wants to be known, he's dark—browned by the sun, a shade of brown that's almost gold, his eyes and teeth flash with brightness, his sun-bleached hair falls below his shoulders, uncut since the Beatles at the Bowl

the other two, Brownie and Bear, descriptions as well as names, they take the bike from me, murmuring affirmations, "it's all right, you can let go, we've got it—" they lower the back of the pickup, pull a plank down to make a ramp, the two of them are stronger than they look, they wheel the hog up the ramp and into the back of the truck, I dont remember anyone asking, I'm too drained to protest

Brownie helps me up into the back of the truck, next to the bike, there's lumber and canvas, assorted tools and cardboard boxes, everything piled neatly, and a mattress too, Brownie tells me to lie down, Bear and Shine get in front and we're rolling down the road, a bumpy ride, the pickup has no shocks and the road has gone years without repair, I stare up at the painful blue sky, feeling lost and dizzy, feeling as if I'm falling up into it

an hour, maybe more, probably less, I fade in and out, we're on a dirt road now, bumpy and uncomfortable, eventually we arrive somewhere, but we're still in Arizona, every place in Arizona looks like every other place, burnt red rocks and empty desert, and no matter what you build, or how shiny you make it, everything still looks ephemeral, like a cardboard house waiting only for the first big wind to hurl it off to Neverland or Oz or who cares where, a year from now, a hundred years, the desert will still be here, you wont but it will

this place, this empty place, a scramble of willpower against entropy, still had a haphazard sense of desperate order, like a careless scattering of ideas—we rattled around a lean-to made of ancient scraps of lumber and sheet metal, and pulled up next to a teepee of weathered canvas, a first-american mansion, behind it a water-tank sideways on a concrete bed, maybe something leftover from the construction of the road, except there was no road here, only a broad garden and a ramp leading down to a dugout with a roof of planks and canvas, the cheapest possible shelter, and sturdiest against the howling winds that swept across the desert at night

they walk me into the teepee and sit me down, lay me down, and in a minute I'm surrounded by beautiful young men pulling my clothes off me and washing me down with cool wet cloths, and either I'm hallucinating or I've found the western version of Mama-San's Happy House, except it's neither or both, I'm not hallucinating and this isnt Mama's either, but it's a place and it's real and if there's a God, a discussion I can argue either side of, she dropped me here for a reason, and if there isnt then the true nature of coincidence defies logic, but I already knew that, I came back, not everyone did—all of me except one leg, which is a lot more than a lot of guys came back with

it was the seventies, we never got to San Francisco and the flowers wilted before we could put them in our hair, all the beads and silliness got turned into plastic exercises in style, the movement colonized and coopted by Hollywood poseurs, people with typewriters and cameras trying to sell us what was ours to begin with, we should have seen it coming, but in our naivete we flipped the record over, took another toke and said shit like "groovy" and "heavy, man" and ended up with missing pieces, not just legs and arms and sometimes dicks, but too many parts that didnt show

I got off the plane in San Francisco—and no, nobody spat on me, that was a myth, a story, a piece of bullshit propaganda, a convenient lie so we could hate the libbies—but I stripped out of my uniform in the first restroom I passed, shoved it back into my duffel, the duffel gave me away anyway, that and the leg and the cane

spent a drunken weekend in a Folsom Street bath house, not for the fucking, but because I could stand in the hot shower for endless hours, steam-cleaning myself, a desperate attempt to scourge away the last stink of the Delta, a stench that lingered in my brain long after my skin had turned lobster-red

some of the guys looked at me, stumping down the hallways on one good leg and one plastic one, wondering perhaps if I would take it off when or if we did the horizontal illusion of affection

in those first days back, I was still lean and hard, inside and out, especially inside, and I had that look, the "dont fuck with me" look, if youve seen it you know what it looks like and if you havent seen it then you havent met me, but that was what they saw, so yeah—nobody fucked with me, except the ones who wanted me to fuck with them, and after the first three or four, I figured it out, those were the ones I didnt want to fuck with, they were just bodies, inhabited by desperate hungry things, sucking at other people's power, six inches at a time, because they didnt have any of their own, they were users, wanting to be used so they could use you back in their own way

that wasnt what I wanted, hell, I didnt know what I wanted, but I knew this wasnt it, and sometime Monday I stumped out into the daylight, blinking at how bright it was, still stinking inside, you cant wash away that stink, no matter how many showers you take, no matter how much dope you smoke, it's part of you, now and forever, and you cant fuck it away, fucking gives you maybe at best thirty seconds of forgetting, that's it

so I bought the hog and started riding, I didnt know what I was looking for, so I wouldnt know what it was if I found it, but whatever it was, I wasnt going to find it where I was because I'd already been here and it wasnt here either, so I bought the hog and started riding, it seemed like a good idea, it made sense at the time

eventually ending up on that ugly Arizona slab, ten or twenty, thirty thousand miles later, sliding into the dirt, pushing the hog uphill even on the downslope, the scorching heat soaking into the steel of the machine, I'm wearing hot leather gloves so I dont barbecue myself on the handlebars, and I dont dare stop, because if I do I'll never start again, and just when I was starting to realize I was probably going to die out here and what a fucking waste that would be, that's when the angels arrived in a battered red Chevy pickup

they had to be angels, they glowed

it was everything about them, the way they stood, tall and easy and self-assured, they all had this crazy calm sense of being, a kind of quiet peace—they didn't say much, it was like they already knew what to do, each one taking his part of the job without having to be told—and something else, they looked alive and confident—like they knew something that the rest of us didnt

it's the look you want to see, not the look you get, the look that should have been there, but wasn't—

in the middle of the boom-boom, lying face down in the mud and blood and dirty ditch water, preparing to drown until somebody rolled me over, and the bright blue dome of dazzle startled the cough out of me, a wide-eyed terrified corpsman screaming, "I got it! I got it!" while frantically doing something to my leg, a tourniquet something, and then the bite of the needle—I blissed out until I was bounced awake again, staring at the dirty roof of the truck, and somebody saying, "lucky piece of shit just bought a ticket home—"

high price to pay for a ticket and long trip to nowhere, too long—even longer to get a leg that fits—the machinery chugs and churns, here's another piece of meat to be cured and shipped, keep it calm and cooperating, so we wont have to take the blame—all the plastic faces, all wearing the same detached expression, the hollow reassuring smile, professional and uncaring—and all of them, they go home at night while I wheel myself around the ward, listening to the screaming and the sobbing of the guys who came back with less than me, so I cant even feel sorry for myself, just angry

and now the Arizona replay, not as bad, but just as bad in a different way, only this time no morphine and a different flavor of heat, dry instead of wet, coughing up dust and sweat instead of mud and blood, except no—these boys, these beautiful lean boys, they're angels, they glow

something in the tea they gave me, probably,

I faded in and out for a day and a night, someone kept putting a straw in my mouth, something to suck—eventually, I woke up, sat up, looked up, looked around, I was naked, only a sheet, a soft blanket kicked off at the foot of the not-a-bed, just a mattress

he sat opposite, legs crossed, watching, waiting patiently, he wore only a loincloth, he brushed his brown hair away from his eyes. "Welcome back. Welcome to the 'mune—" he pointed to the sky, "not the moon—" then he pointed to the earth, "the *'mune*," he said it just a little differently, "and we're the 'mune-men. That sounds better than 'that pack of crazy faggots out in the desert'—that's what the townies call us—hi, everyone calls me Red." He poured tea into a dark brown bowl, not a mug, passed it across with both hands, very ceremonial

enough time, bouncing around Asia, you learn that everything is a ceremony, I took the bowl with both hands, nodded, inhaled deeply the steam rising from it, recognized the scent of tea, but there were other things in it as well, it would be rude to ask

a sip, just a sip, an odd flavor, but not unpleasant, a bit of spice, but something else, I looked across at Red—

"There's nothing in it," he reassured me. "Nothing narcotic. We dont believe in messing with people's heads, and certainly not their brain chemistry. We're about health here. Inner and outer."

"I've heard that before—" I caught myself before I said more, this wasn't the place.

"I'm sure you have. There are people who use that word to describe a lot of things that aren't. This place—" He indicated the 'mune with a spreading movement of both hands, a very Buddha-like gesture, but he didnt have the body for it, no fat, all burnt away in the glare, just lean brown muscle. "—This place isn't about what you get, it's about what you give." I must have looked confused, because he added,

"Brownie and Bear are repairing your motorcycle. They took the engine apart to clean it. Shine has driven into Tucson to pick up parts. He'll be back tomorrow. You will be on your way a day or two after that. In the meantime, is there somewhere you need to be? Someone you have to call? We dont have a phone, but we have a ham radio, I can power up the generator—"

I shook my head. "I was just—just riding. Nowhere in particular. Why did your friends stop for me?"

"If they hadn't stopped, you would have died."

"I been through worse."

Red glanced at my leg. "Probably. But just the same, if they hadn't stopped, you would have died."

"I dont get it. Why are they fixin' my bike?"

"Why not? They wanted the challenge. And we can't leave you stranded, can we?"

"Sure you can. You wouldn't be the first—"

"It wouldn't be right—"

"I can't pay you—"

"Did we ask you to? Do you want more tea? How are you feeling?"

"I gotta piss real bad."

"That's good. It means you're not dehydrated. Come on—" He helped me to my feet, "I'll show you the men's room. It's outside."

For a moment, Red studied my nakedness. "You want something to wear? Naked is fine too. But you can burn real quick out here." He offered a long open shirt, a mismatched pair of shorts, some very light material, it made sense in this heat, I ducked out of the teepee after, following him past a garden where a couple more lanky boys, shirtless and brown, were hoeing weeds, they waved a greeting, I waved back, why not—we followed a ceramic pipe, a makeshift aqueduct, down a slope to somewhere downwind, a compost pit, spotted with ironic sunflowers and assorted other botanic volunteers. Red pointed,

"Here—"

"Here?"

"Here."

I'd seen better latrines in the Delta, dug a few myself, but this was different—this was that thing they called recycling, giving back to the earth what you were taking out of it

dump your garbage here, everything from egg shells to coffee grounds, orange and banana peels, onion skins, apple cores, everything biodegradable, and wash water and runoff, all the sewage too, everything that helps make healthy topsoil—pee here, poop here, toss a few shovels of dirt on top to slow down the stink and the insects, every so often get in there with a pitchfork, knock the volunteers down, and turn everything over, when the worms are big enough to fight back, it's ready for the garden—

I'd peed in worse places, I'd shit there too, places with names, places without—

Red said, "The limit isn't the topsoil, it's the water, there isn't enough. But we're working on it. Bear graduated engineering school, Brownie dropped out, they're designing a thing to extract water from the air—over there, that's one of their experiments—" A tall framework with sheets of Saran-Wrap stretched diagonally to catch the overnight dew, sliding the drops into waiting pots before the heat of the day turned them back into vapor. "It works but not enough, water still has to be trucked in two-three times a month, sometimes more than that. We'll probably never have enough water to grow our own rice, but we've got beans and tomatoes and corn, eventually we'll be self-sufficient. That's the goal anyway. In the meantime, we pick up work here and there. Sometimes we haul trash for the locals. Half the stuff we have, someone else threw out. Out there—they're all living in the Age of Waste. Here, we're learning how to survive without waste."

"Why?"

Red looked sad, he smiled and looked sad, both at the same time, and I felt embarrassed for asking the question. "Because you have to ask. That's why."

"Oh."

Something was bothering me. "Those motorcycle parts. They're not cheap. I'll pay for 'em. Next disability check. I'm good for it—"

Red shook his head. "No. Keep your money."

"Eh?" I frowned.

"Money is slavery."

That made no sense. I blurted words automatically. "Who made up that bullshit?"

"You did—when you decided that your time was for sale."

I started to—and then stopped, thought about what he'd said, thought about it from his side—money as enslavement, okay, yeah—it's supposed to be a measure of the value of work, but we turn it into something else, a measure of our own value, that's when it ties us up and it ties us down. I hadnt thought about it his way, but I saw the point. "Right. So what can I do to work it off?"

He shook his head. He focused on my eyes, his look sparkled. "No. Not work—"

I held out my hands between us, rough and scarred, callused and still dirty from the bike. "This is all I've got."

"That's enough. Just dont call it work."

"Why not?"

Red got serious now. "Work—that used to be something honorable, something to take pride in. Now—people talk about work like they hate it. They've made the word ugly. Work is something they dont want to do, but they *have* to do, every day, just to survive. The whole day is spent being unhappy. That's not life, that's not being really alive, is it?"

"But you still gotta do it—"

"Do you? Do you see us working here?"

"I haven't seen anything yet."

"We dont work. We contribute."

My face must have shown my reaction to the word 'contribute' because his sparkle faded. "Have to tell ya, Red. That sounds like a big fat crock of San Francisco jargon, that's why I left that city—"

He shrugged, a kind of agreement. "Yeah, it does sound like it. Those folks in San Francisco—they're trying, y'know. The best they can. Change the language, shift the context, transform the experience—yeah, it sounds like they're speaking Martian, but they're trying. Give 'em credit for that. In the end, we're all fumbling with the future, aren't we?"

"Okay, I won't call it work. If that'll make you happy. I'll … contribute. What can I do for you guys? What do you need?"

"Look around." He waved. "What do you think?"

"You guys need everything, I mean—" I started thinking, listing in my head all the stuff the sergeants would have assigned. "There's a lot of stuff to do here. Maybe dig a well, if the water table is high enough, build a windmill, I dunno—what do you want? How much work—contribution, whatever you call it—is fair?"

"Whatever you think your time is worth. We won't take advantage of anyone."

Had to think I about that—what I'd earned here and there, doing this, doing that, not all of it legal, what was I worth, to me, to others, hard to say, okay, five per hour seemed fair, weigh that against the price of parts and labor, I didnt know how bad the damage was, not yet, so I couldnt know how much, but even if it wasnt a lot, it was still more than I had, at least here there was food and roof, I should work that off too, and maybe even a bit of sex if that was the vibe I was getting off Red—

"A couple weeks, okay? I got no place else to be. But I can do more if you need."

He put his hand on my shoulder, not a casual touch, he let his fingers slide down toward my heart, what was he looking for? "Only give what you want to freely give. After that, it's not freely given." His fingers lingered—

I missed it, or maybe I didnt, or maybe he was trying to communicate something else, sometimes I'm too stupid for my own good—"I'll do what I can, but dont expect me to stay too long, I dont stay anywhere anymore—" My words must have stung, because Red pulled his hand away. "—but I'll do my piece and I'll do a bit more for good measure, okay?"

Red shrugged. "Do what you will, dont do what you won't."

I did stay, longer than I intended—long until longer, I'd be there now if it was still there, wrapped in Red's arms if I could, but it's long gone, and I blame Sterge and Shine and all the others, but most of all I blame myself and I blame the avalanche of time

see, the Arizona night is—you can see the stars, you can see the Milky Way stretched across the sky like a veil of desire, and it's like you're a piece of it, a very small piece, almost insignificant, but you're the piece the universe created so it could see itself this way

and that's a precious moment, if you're smart enough to notice it when it happens, sometimes you just look up and say, "oh, wow, lookit the stars—" like that's the moment, but it isnt, you gotta look beyond that, you gotta look a thousand, ten thousand, a hundred thousand light years out

all those little blinking glimmering pinpoints, diamonds on black velvet, each one of them a gigantic blazing flaming ball of hydrogen desperately trying to burn itself out and explode, sending shock waves hurtling, light and heat and atoms forged in nuclear fire—and here I am, this little ambulatory bag of water, a sack of protoplasm on a speck of dust a gazillion miles away, just a smidge of that blazing light strikes the receptors at the back of my retina—having traveled across distances so vast, it takes thousands of years to complete the journey, only to flicker for the briefest of instances before the trailing multitude of sibling particles come rushing in after to flicker in their own turn brief moments, and if I werent here, right here in this moment, in this place at this time, then those photons would strike the baked desert sand unseen, as if they had never existed at all, so in that instant, I am the purpose of those particles, I am the reason for their journey, because it was my job to see them and know them and celebrate the astonishing circumstance of their existence—and my own as well, as the random recipient of that tiny sparkle of light—and if the best I can do is say, "oh, wow, lookit the stars—" I'm an idiot, a moron, a naked chimpanzee scrabbling in the dirt, failing to grasp the gift of cosmic perspective that is just waiting for me to recognize it, all I have to do is look up and wonder at the sheer incomprehensible vastness of that panorama stretched across the bright black dome of the cold Arizona night

it pinned me to the spot, stuck me as firmly as a nail-gun, who could walk away, ride away, from this?—not me, I'm the piece the universe created so it could look at itself like this

and in that moment, I wasnt alone

all the other souls that had gathered here, a strange assortment, as if the dice of time had rolled and tossed out the most ill-considered collection of men, and yet

it worked, somehow

we'd sit in a circle around the fire pit, by ones or

twos or threes, never more than nine of us, or maybe once in a while eleven, always an odd number, why was that? Or did it just happen that way? Red said it was part of the mystery—

"What mystery?" I asked.

"The mystery is that we dont know what mystery."

it almost made sense

Shine had a guitar, Caleb had a thing like a keyboard that he'd built himself, Van had a steeldrum he'd made from an old metal garbage can, and we had music—not the three-chord iambic that passed for rock, something else, a whole other language of sound, later on—when other people started recording it, they called it new age and minimalist and trance and a lot of other things, but it wasnt any of that, it was us, it was ours, it was the soul of the desert speaking through us, it was the way we tuned ourselves to each other

an assortment of lanky boys came and went, but seven of us were here all week, long and thin and sinewy, I was even getting there myself, stumping around, hoeing, digging, taking some things apart, building others

depending on mood and weather and time of day, Van wore only a loincloth, Caleb wore less than that unless there were strangers around, he wasnt ashamed, but some people couldnt talk to a naked man easily, not unless they took their own clothes off, and some did, some didnt—I wore the shorts and shirt Red gave me, I wasnt brown enough yet for the desert sun, a couple of the others—they would have had a hard time in places where the sins of the confederacy still echoed

Arizona bakes the fat out of everyone, unless they have air conditioning—it's the difference between crispy bacon and uncooked, you can tell who's uncooked, you can tell who's hiding from the sun and the heat and the desert, sometimes they come out, the curiosity seekers, the adventurers, the ones who've read too many of the wrong books, they stop, they get out of their shining cars with strange expressions on their faces, they look around for a bit, they see there's no ice water, no indoor plumbing, and too many opportunities to burn away the poundage, and they start to realize the size of the chasm they'd have to leap across to get here, how much they'd have to give up, starting with those shining cars—most of 'em are pretty enough, but you can see how distant they are, how far they've been separated from the earth, isolated from the struggle of pulling survival out of the land, they're not lazy, they just dont know, terrified to learn, because all that easy technology has spoiled their ability to connect, not all, but too many—

others understood, or at least they had a glimmer, some of those boys lived in town, only coming out on weekends, usually carrying cartons of supplies and beer, always welcome, but there was that thing—they had jobs, work, the stuff they did so they could have a life on weekends, so that was part of the mystery—the 'mune survived, not because it was self-sufficient, but because it was on life support

but it was a safe place, a place where the town boys could lie down with one another, be together under the stars, taste each other's kisses, be themselves for a while, before heading back into the world of flickering neon promises

we circled every night, arms looped lazily around each other's shoulders—or not, depending on who had the most warmth to share and who needed it most, the smoldering stones kept the last beans of dinner warm, and we'd pass a joint, sometimes a homebrew, and we'd reinvent ourselves, and yeah, there was sex and drugs, mostly on the weekends, mostly the townies, but the ones who lived at the 'mune—those were the ones who *were* the 'mune

there was a ritual, Shine called it "setting context"—he'd share a thought, a starting point for discussion—a question, not an answer, and we'd mull it over, chew it around, holding it up to the light and looking at it from every angle, most of them different ways of asking the same question—what does it mean to be queer in this world?—but the way he said it, it always came out different—like, why do we have to consider ourselves queer, why do we make that distinction, what does it mean to be a man, what is the fundamental relationship between one man and another, and how can we take care of each other? Stuff I never talked about before because it was stuff I never thought about before—

because that was the thing, the whole reason the 'mune existed—all the things we didnt speak aloud, because we didn't know how, nobody did, but yeah, it was always there—how much we'd all been beaten up and beaten down, all those whispered conversations, furtive and embarrassed, except when they were loud and ugly, and the looks, the hate stares, ignorance working itself into a blather, a conspiracy of bullshit telling us who we had to be, who we shouldn't be, who we could never be, and worst of all, who we couldnt love—all that noise about how our kind of love wasnt possible, it was sick and immoral and degenerate and perverse and also illegal—so we walked around pretending to be something we werent and fooling no one except ourselves, and that was the point—this place, this 'mune was a flicker of possibility, a chance to redefine and reinvent and just breathe the clean desert air without being hammered by other people's flabbering yaps

except—what they were trying to do here, these glowing boys, nobody had ever been there before, it was an undiscovered continent, no road map, maybe a few animal trails, but even the little bit they'd already accomplished, it was a start—

if only

see, they weren't just

there was a point

one evening at the circle

I didnt even realize it myself, not until Red put his hand on my leg, leaned over and said, "Did you notice? You're not saying 'you guys' any more. You're saying 'us guys.'"

oh—

how did that happen? When did I—

I guess it happened when I started feeling—

whatever it was I was feeling

okay, but yeah, if we knew what we were doing, we would have done it, but we didnt know, we were stumbling, fumbling, bumbling our way toward someplace called enlightenment, or someplace that looked like it, we wouldnt know until we got there, because we werent just reinventing ourselves, we were reinventing the whole idea of reinventing, and nobody had ever done this before, or if anybody had we didn't know, so we sat and talked and shared and because Shine kept hammering at us, we hammered at the language because language was everything, it was all we had, and if we didnt own it then it would own us, it made sense after a while, you had to live with it—or inside of it—but anyway that was the way you set the context

Shine talked about context a lot, he said context is everything—he said, "I had an uncle who lived in California, Hollywood—not the glamor, just the factory that produces it—after he burned out, he came to live with us for a while. One night, he and my dad had a big fight, I dont remember what it was about, but I remember something he shouted. He said a lot of things, but the one I remember was when he said, 'Indiana is boring. Not the state. The people.' Later on, when he was packing to move out, I went to him and asked him if we were really boring.

"He sat down next to me on the bed and apologized. No, Indiana isnt boring, the people arent boring. He'd spoken out of turn. But that wasnt a good enough answer for me. I asked him what he meant. Finally, he admitted that where he'd come from, everyone lived made-up lives. One day you were a cowboy, the next you were an astronaut. One day you were a cop, the next you were a murderer. One day you were living in the past, the next you were living in the future. Everybody was always making up new lives. It didnt matter if you were a writer or an actor or a director or a costumer or a whatever, every day you were living in a different time and place, so you had to learn how to think a lot of different ways and be a lot of different kinds of people. But in Indiana, there's only one way to be, only one life to live, and...yeah, if you came from a place where you had to be someone else every day, then yeah, being the same person day after day would be boring."

he said that was the day he started wondering—why do you have to be the same person every day, what if you could reinvent yourself whenever you wanted

when he realized he couldn't be one of the people who lived in Indiana, he left—he rolled west blown by that same strange wind that blows all the weirdest and craziest people west, until finally they stop because if they rolled any further, they'd drown—you ever been to Venice beach?

but Shine was different, he ended up in Berkeley, he was there for the riots, he stayed on because it was a fermenting stewpot of ideas—he studied Hermeneutics and General Semantics and Neuro-Linguistic Programming and even some weird seminar series at the Jack Tar Hotel in San Francisco where they called you an asshole and wouldnt let you pee—until he dropped out of school, or maybe got kicked out, he didnt say, but somewhere along the way he picked up the word "reinvention" and it had triggered some kind of epiphany—one night, naked in bed with two other guys, maybe a little too stoned, talking even more than fucking, they decided to reinvent themselves, the first escapees from the Age of Waste, eventually, after a couple weeks of discussion, and a couple more weeks working up the courage to commit, they loaded up a VW van and drove as far as they could on a tank of gas, ending up in Arizona, trading the van for a dozen uninhabitable acres of baked sand and clay, possibly not the smartest decision, the guy who got the van was able to leave

but yeah, a little of this, a little of that, a lot of work—contribution—every day, others heard and came by, some stayed and played, some didnt, some came whenever they could get away, weekends were always busy—over time the bits and pieces started to come together, not just the 'mune, but the men who lived there as well—it wasnt paradise, but it wasnt supposed to be, it was penance

it was cleansing, it was scourging, it was recovery, it was healing, it was all that before it could even start to be reinvention

only you dont/cant see it that way until afterward, until you get to the other side and look back and see how far you've come

for me, for the longest time, it was about digging

first the compost pit

it's a dirty job, but somebody's gotta do it—old joke, yeah, but in this case, a measure of commitment too, are you willing to get dirty, are you committed to being dirty if that's what's wanted and needed

me, I didnt care, I'd been dirtier—compared to the blood and shit I'd crawled through, compost is chocolate pudding—compost is healthy, it's life, it's all those little fungal processes of decay silently turning garbage into topsoil, but you gotta know what kind of garbage to mix, lettuce leaves, onions, coffee grounds, egg shells, dryer lint, chicken bones, yeah—that would be good, if we had any of that stuff, but no—we've got beanstalks and corn husks, shit and piss and noodles that no one finished, that's okay, no prob, we've also got gray water from washing things down and too often that's got motor oil and grease and other crap in it, stuff you dont want in the ground, so what do we do with that shit, cant even burn it, that just puts the toxins in the air—but that's just taking the dirt and moving it somewhere else

Shine talked about that a lot, there's no such thing as cleaning, there's just relocating stuff, taking it from one place to another, think about it, you dont get rid of the trash, you just put it in the can for someone else to carry away, what do they do with it—they dump it somewhere in great big piles, mountains of it—our problem is that we concentrate our dirt, making it ever more toxic, and that's the question Shine wanted to answer, how can we reuse our own shit instead of piling it up in more mountains—if all we have is shit, we can grow things, but what about the shit that isnt just shit, it's poison

and no, we didnt have the answer, I dont know if there is one—what keeps archaeologists in business is sorting through trash heaps a thousand, two thousand years old—in all that time, we still havent learned anything about the shit we pile up around us

and especially not the shit we pile up inside us

that's the problem, I can move it around from one place to another all I want, I can play patty-cake with that shit till my eyes bleed, but it doesnt matter where I move it to, it's still inside my head

the mind-mice gnaw at the base of my skull

no escape, no exit

the best I can do is bury myself

digging in the hot sun, maybe I can bake some of that shit out, maybe I can burn off some of the fat, maybe I can earn a place with these lean lanky boys, maybe I can stop hurting long enough to remember—no, not remember, because I never knew—long enough to discover all that joyous shit that everyone says life is supposed to be about

the days blur, one into the next, we smoke, we joke, and I turn brown, still hard, but once in a while someone holds up a mirror and my eyes are flashing bright, I'm getting a little bit of the glow, even almost a hint of a smile, go figure

but yeah, I began to understand the glow—no, not understand—Shine says understanding is the booby prize, you have to live it to get it, the explanation is the menu, not the meal—all that crapola jargon, it only makes sense afterward

so the glow, yeah

you couldnt say what it was, because there wasnt anything specific about it, but it was there and you could see it—it was just something that showed up different

details, yeah—okay, the lanky boys didnt slouch, they didnt frown—well, only if they were struggling for a moment with something difficult, but mostly not, mostly they laughed—the more difficult something became, the more they laughed about it, "man, this thing is tough" with the unspoken addition "but I'm tougher"

there wasnt that lost sense, that feeling of stumbling blindly through the day, from one meal to the next, we could go into town on an errand and people would look at us, they saw we were different, you could see their faces pucker up, like we were supposed to be the same as they were, beaten up and beaten down—and maybe we had been once, some of us a lot more than any human being should ever have to endure, but we'd left it behind whatever it was we had, I had only the smallest piece of it, but it was enough, like getting a piece of really nice birthday cake, it might be someone else's cake, but I had a share of it too

I didnt go into town that much, it made me uncomfortable, the disapproving way the locals would look at us, as if their faces hurt from the inside—the sideways frowns, the hasty look-aways, the hate-stares, or worse, the ones who didnt look at all, they just mumbled along oblivious

and some of them, especially the younger ones, you could see it in their eyes, the longing, the hurt, the hunger, they'd look at us and you knew they wanted us, they wanted what we were, they wanted—something

if not to join us, then at least to *know* what the fuck it was we were doing out there in the desert that made us glow

it was life, we were alive, it showed

sometimes they just wanted to fuck us, one way or another, you learned to read faces, body language, you learned real fast, you learned not to go into town on weekends, and you learned not to speak to any of them unless you had to, not to be too loud, and not to be anything at all

I felt sorry for them, because they didnt know, couldnt know, I wanted to take them aside and tell them what was possible, but I couldnt, because I could already see it in their faces, they didnt know how to believe it, the same way I hadnt known how to believe it

that was in town

in the desert—I didnt know the desert could be so funny—we spent a lot of time laughing

not at jokes, unless the joke was ourselves

no, we laughed with delight at the beauty of the striations in the red rocks, we laughed at the clouds that streaked across the western sky, the red and ochre mountains, the pink and purple shades across the silent firestorm of sunset, the way a jackrabbit or a roadrunner scrambled across the sand, anything, we laughed because we were alive, the joke was on us, the universe had dropped us here and given us this beauty to enjoy or ignore—and if we were stupid enough to ignore it, then we were just assholes

except—we already knew we were assholes, that was the joke, that was why we laughed, we were assholes because we were human, and because the whole human race, every single one of us, we're all assholes, compressing our souls into little tiny nuggets of bitterness and then taking it out on each other as if it's someone else's fault that we're assholes

when you get the joke, you're still an asshole, except now you know it and that's even funnier

and if you dont get the joke, then you're still an asshole

one day, I got the joke

The bike was fixed, long fixed, I was brown as a bean, lean and hard, and one cold morning the sky was so blue it ached, the horizon was clear enough to touch, and I realized I'd stayed here too long, overstayed, was turning into someone I didnt recognize

that last visit to town, it stirred up memories, hungers, dissatisfactions—there were things I was missing, burgers and beer, television and bars, even the occasional fistfight, all that stuff that we gave up so arrogantly—but most of all, the road, those gleaming white highways, the superslab that ribboned from here to everywhere, I couldnt stay here, I couldnt stay anywhere for long, I'd never had a home, wasnt going to start now

the bike gleamed like cool blue metal, it hadn't warmed up yet, but soon enough—every so often, I'd lever myself onto it, start it up, run the engine, just to hear the sound, just to keep the battery charged I told myself, but mostly to feel that bear-like rumble between my legs, that vibration of lust and speed and power—only today, it was different, sitting on the bike, sitting atop three thousand fiery explosions per minute, revving it up to five or six just to watch the needle spike—and off in the distance, the crisp new mountains, and suddenly I wanted to see what was on the other side

it was the town, the locals, their shut down faces, the ugly disapproval, it scared me—not scared like fear, but scared like awakened—I wanted to get away from that ugliness, I had a feeling, a hunch, a disturbing premonition that I was suddenly living on the edge of a bubble about to burst, and if it did I'd hurt like I'd never hurt before—and I didnt even think about it, I grabbed my gear, strapped it to the back of the bike and roared and bounced toward the two-lane, like a screaming bat out of the place beneath Hell

and I dont know how far I got, fifty—a hundred miles—before I pulled off to the side of the road, skidding and screeching, swerving across the sand until I rolled to a stop and fell off the bike and started sobbing, great wracking gasps of anguish, because I knew why I was running away—because I was scared, scared of caring too much, scared of caring so much it would hurt if nobody cared back, I'd never felt like that ever before in my life, and it was the most uncomfortable disconcerting burning cold chill in my gut that I'd ever known, because there was no reason why I should ever feel this way about anyone, I'd turned off caring a long time ago and

oh fuck, oh fuck, oh fuck, oh fuck

it was too late, I did care, and I couldnt stand this feeling

I sat there on the sand, the hot burning sand, not caring that my ass was getting scorched, watching the occasional truck roar by, the Mustangs and the Camaros, tops down, blond boys heading off to anywhere but here

and laughed

because I was a jerk, an asshole, an idiot

eventually, I got back up on the bike, started the engine again, and headed back to the 'mune, the dark side of the 'mune, only now there was a bright side too, hell yeah, because now I got the joke and I didnt have to look in the mirror to see how brightly I was glowing because

—it happened—

and when I rolled back up the road, letting the bike coast in the last few feet, there was Red and Shine, Brownie and Bear, Caleb and Van, and they looked up from the fire pit and waved, and when I dismounted and went over to join them, nobody said anything at all that I'd been gone all day, Red slid his hand across and down my back, a reassuring stroke, just the same he did every night

"Did you go anyplace interesting?"

"No. Just for a ride. Just needed to blow some stink out of my head."

"That's good. I'm glad you're back. I missed you."

"Yeah, I missed you too."

So Red and I, yeah—it happened, not that night, but yeah—it happened

first I had to flush a lot of bad shit out of my head

and I didnt know how to do that

after the fire died down, after the others had crawled off to wherever, disappearing into their separate beds, alone or together, I never really noticed, Red and I were the last ones sitting, he looked at me, he slipped his hand in mine, an easy smile, he said, "let's take a walk" and I stood up with him and

went with him—out into the cold desert, away from the glow of the camp, just the two of us, holding hands under the bright stars, the whispering veil of the Milky Way, occasional shooting stars flashing across the sky, once even a fiery meteor

he didnt have to say anything, he didn't have to ask, I just started talking, first about nothing, then about something, and finally about everything

I told him the truth, how I had gotten on the bike intending to leave and not come back, I told him how I'd ridden blindly, unconsciously, easily falling into that bad old habit of letting the road hypnotize me into thinking I was going somewhere, realizing suddenly, I was only going nowhere, skidding off the road to sit in a big puddle of ache

he listened, he listened with his eyes, he listened with his whole body, he listened hungrily, as if every word I said was worth a bucket of clean water and he was going to shower in it, bathe in it, swim in it

and when I was done, when I ran out of things to say, when I ran out of words, I just stopped in the middle of a sentence, my voice trailing off into a whisper and then nothingness, an echo of meaning

Red faced me, studied me, looked at me so intensely I couldnt look away, didnt dare, and then grinning, he pulled me into his arms and held me so tight there was no escape, I didnt want to anyway, and we just stood there for the longest time, him wearing only his loincloth and me still in my jeans and T-shirt, so my hands slid up and down his naked skin, at first searching for the right place to hold him, and then wondering if he was cold in this night air and if I had to warm him up, and finally just to appreciate the sheer smooth beauty of his body, and yeah—I couldnt speak, my throat was dry and tight and my eyes were aching in a way I couldnt recognize, I just held on, never wanting to let go, and it wasnt just because he felt good—he felt better than anybody—no, it was because I didnt want to let go because I didn't want to feel alone again

"It's all right, Chase," he finally whispered, "I'm here, I'm not going away, I'm not letting go."

I wished I could believe that, but I didnt believe anything anymore, no matter how much I wished I could—I didnt believe because I didnt trust, and I'd probably never trust again

that's what I brought back from Nam—suspicion, fear, anger, hatred, grief, rage, and those are just the tip of it, because the rest are things that nobody has named yet because nobody's gone down deep enough to see and survived long enough to report back—but trust wasnt one of the things anyone brought back

because if you couldnt trust yourself, you couldnt trust anyone else either

so no, I just stood there holding Red, not speaking, because speaking would have made it real again and I'd had too much of that reality already

I dont know how long we stood there, it could have been a minute, an hour, forever—the moment was timeless—but at last, finally, I noticed Red was shivering and we broke apart, I pulled off my T-shirt and handed it to him, he tugged it on, and we walked back, my arm around his shoulder, holding him close, and we fell together into his bed, not for sex, but only to keep each other warm

and that was how things went for a day, a week, a little longer than that, I lost track of time, didnt care, went back to digging, digging was good for me, stumping around in the dirt—I had to learn to walk again after they gave me the metal and plastic leg, the damn thing was heavy, so I learned a new gait, a kind of a swing and limp, it almost looked normal, but in the dirt, on the sand, I had to learn another kind of movement, until it became so easy I never noticed it anymore, and after a while, it was just the way I was, and in the evening, getting ready for bed, unstrapping the damn thing, I didnt even resent it anymore, it was just what it was, part of me and one night, sitting there, rubbing the stump, rubbing life back into the leg, Red came over and said, "let me," and he began rubbing my leg, and somehow his hands found their way north of there to my own delta and

yeah

it was good

he didnt ask for more than he was willing to give and he gave everything he had, so I had to do the same, it took me a while, but he was patient and I was—whatever I was—but it worked

and life was good for a while, there were things I could do and things I couldnt do, but I did the things I could and that was enough, more than enough—turned out I was better at cooking than I thought, better than some of the guys, I'd learned a bit here and there, and I liked doing it—there's a zone, a focus, a narrowing of the moment where time and space all collapse down to the place where the knife slides through the onion or the tomato or the potato, laying precise even pieces across the cutting board, and the particular rhythm of the action, the precise intention of purpose, it all comes together in an ephemeral culmination—the hearty belch at the end of the meal, the grunts of satisfaction, the chorus of voices, "yeah, that was good"—and coalesces into a feeling of quiet accomplishment, challenge met, challenge won, let's do it again tomorrow—there are things you can do with corn and tomatoes, beans and rice, a little bit of pepper, some potatoes, maybe some cheese and onions, eggs if you got 'em, and a healthy spice cabinet, nobody starves, nobody complains

Red and I became a thing—okay, a couple—it was never official, it was just what it was, an understanding that he and I would always end up in the same bed, even when the weekend boys arrived, we didnt talk much, he didnt have much to say, I had too much I wouldnt say, but we werent that much apart, he'd didnt have much family either, so maybe that was why we both held onto each other so intensely

he'd walked away from mommy and daddy's suburban fantasy—thrown out maybe, or maybe exiting before the mandatory eviction, he never said it in words, but the way he didn't say it, I got it anyway—hitchhiked out into the desert, aiming for a mythical oasis he'd read about in a magazine, ending up at the 'mune, nervous and eager and desperate—by the time I arrived, he'd stopped hurting so loudly, but I guess the scars still ached, I know mine did, he was lean and tight and we fit together, at least I thought we did—well, we did for that little while, I have to believe that

because

in the middle of the night, the huge empty darkness, the sprawling stars, the biting wind, we'd wrap ourselves around each other, sometimes desperately holding onto each other like human life preservers, sometimes just spooning—which too often led inevitably to forking, sometimes a frenzied wrestle, but more often a long slow glide of togetherness, a connection that was more spiritual than physical, a sharing of breath and heartbeats, a shared nakedness, flesh against flesh, he desired me as much as I desired him—no, I dont believe in soul mates, not anymore, but for a brief moment there I stopped thinking about tomorrow

that was my mistake

because that's when Sterge arrived

Sterge was possibly the most beautiful man any of us had ever seen, there wasnt anything specifically beautiful about him, and it wasnt even the way the pieces fit together, it was something else—just the way he breathed and spoke and moved

like he had his own personal glow

Sterge wasnt a big guy, but he looked big, he

looked tall, but it was only an inch, maybe two, more than me, it was more in the way he stood, the way he carried himself—he had a narrow face, shaped kind of like an axe, with eyes just as sharp, piercing blue, and underneath, a smile so wide you could fall into it, a bright easy-going smile, y'know— like he's got it, all of it, just tucked away behind those eyes and that happy knowing smile

and when he showed up the guys just melted, I didnt understand why—I mean, I could see the attraction, but at the same time I didnt/couldnt

most of the time, queers dont give it up like that—I mean, maybe when you're still just a little piece of chicken, yeah, your dick goes sproing, and you think that's your heart talking, but mostly it's your dick, and only after you get your heart stomped a few times do you learn not to listen to your dick—you get narrow-eyed

but Sterge showed up, his shirt open unbuttoned, his jeans hanging off his waist, faded bell-bottom jeans, a little frayed, a little ragged, just enough to show he'd lived in 'em long enough to be real, hanging low enough to reveal just enough of that delta vee, where the eyes are sucked into the hint of what's next

but that wasnt the half of it, see—Sterge knew how to work it, he had the looks, he had the eyes, the smile, the smooth chest, with just enough tree-of-life sprinkle of hair to suggest that he could put you on your back and send you to heaven, seven inches at a time

even Shine, who mostly slept alone, was charmed

whatever magic Sterge had, yeah—he brought it big time

me, yeah, I could appreciate what he was, but I didnt want any, I dont know why—something inside me said, no, dont go there, just dont, so I didnt, but—yeah, I listened, we all did, all of us, we couldnt help it, he was—well, he was Sterge, and if you've ever met a Sterge, then you know, and if you've never met one, then no amount of describing is going to make him real

you know all that guru stuff that went on back then, that airy-fairy, touchy-feely, new age crap—it was bullshit, most of it—just a bunch of stuff to get you out of your own head long enough to hear someone say, 'stop being an asshole'—mostly, it was excuse for people to pretend they've found an answer—the I Ching and the enneagram and iridology and rebirthing and rolfing and isolation tanks and from there they went to red-blue pyramid games and sharpening razor blades under pyramids and you cant believe the craziness they were making up about how the universe wanted to believe in us and how prosperity was our divine right

but here came Sterge, with his very own brand of bullshit—home-grown, so it had to be good

and the others had smoked this dream before, so

so I kept my cock-hole shut and went along

maybe they knew something

but it was the glow

it sucked people in, they couldnt help themselves

after you lived in the 'mune for a while, you started to glow, people could see it, they didnt know what it was, but they could see it, and whatever it was, they wanted it—even today, you can look at the old Polaroids and you can see it

so here comes Sterge, the glow vampire—yeah, as near as I could figure it out afterward, he didnt have a glow of his own, he only had what he could suck out of others, he fed on it

Shine missed it, all his talk of eco-systems and such, he thought we were the apex predators, but no—even apex predators have predators, parasites and fleas and lice and rats who live on the scraps and droppings, we had enough of 'em around the 'mune, we shouldnt have been surprised when a few human life-suckers showed up

and we werent, most of the time we were pretty good at spotting the phonies, the leeches, the posers, the users—but Sterge, he was something different, a charismasaur, something so different he traveled in his own charmfield and you had to be dead to be immune

we glowed, he sparkled—that's the only way I can describe it

and yeah, it didnt take long

that first night, anyone's first night, we're always hungry for news, for stories, but Sterge didnt even wait—it was like he had already assumed leadership, he started talking about how what we were doing here, the 'mune, it wasnt just an experiment, it was the bleeding edge of the knife of time

he had this way with words, candid and lyrical, bubbling with magical insights and illusions of enlightenment, visions and inspirations, like the inevitable golden castle in the sky at the end of a Disney movie, Prince Charming sweeps you away and rides you off to the bright pink fantasy of happily ever after—that was Sterge, you felt good for listening, but just like cotton candy, there was nothing to bite into, just a sugary delusion

yeah, he sucked us in

here, he said, look around, what do you see—

desert, rocks, sand, stars, faces warmed by the fire

no, he said, no—you're missing it, I see the future, I see tomorrow and tomorrow and tomorrow—the human race, he said, we're evolving, look around, see that glow on the horizon, there's a city behind those mountains, for the first time in history, the night is no longer a barrier

no, wait—let me go deeper than that—electricity, telephones, automobiles, radio and television, vaccinations, antibiotics, jet airplanes, rockets, men on the moon, computers, everything—all the stuff that didnt exist a hundred years ago—suddenly we're living in a world of technological possibility, doing things that were unimaginable when our grandparents were born—think of it, in such a short time, we've gone from—from whatever we were before to whatever we are now

but that's only the half of it, all that stuff—transportation, communication, medicine—all that stuff is an ecological force, like ice ages and continental drift and anything else that pushes a species to adapt—all that stuff is going to change us, transform us—and here you are, out here in the Arizona desert, sitting under the stars, already recognizing that, already putting the first pieces together, assembling the next step in human evolution, whatever we're going to become next—there's a word I heard, you'll be hearing a lot of it too—trans-human—that's what you're inventing here, the humanity that will survive in the age of techno-evolution

um, really? I thought we were learning how to live apart from the Age of Waste

Sterge's eyes brightened—yes, that's the point, thank you—he pointed at my leg, I was wearing shorts now, no longer self-conscious—there, see that, your metal and plastic leg, a hundred years ago that wouldnt have been possible, you'd have died on the operating table, or maybe survived, screaming in agony because there were no anesthetics then, and you'd have hobbled around afterward on a crutch, or maybe a wooden peg if you were lucky enough to find one that fit, but no—here you are, walking, working, digging, building, getting on with the business of having a life that works for you, right?

he pointed off toward the horizon—you're not there, you're here—if there's something over there you need, you can go and get it, but you're here, what does that say about you? I'll tell you—it says that you're not them, you dont need them, dont want to be part of them—it says that you're not going to plug into that life, you're going to take only what you need so you can come back out here and plug into this life, plug back into the earth like the true naked animal you are—a naked ape

all of us, naked apes—the difference is, you know it, or at least you're living it on your way to remembering it—and again, he pointed to the horizon, this time derisively—those monkeys, they've not only forgotten it, they're hiding from it, they live in wooden boxes eating food that comes in cardboard boxes, slabs of meat arrive at the fire wrapped in plastic because it came from a factory, pre-drained of the blood and the battle of the hunt—in the morning, those pathetic monkeys get into another box, a metal box with wheels, and drive to a bigger box, all glass and concrete, where they spend the day moving paper from one side of the desk to another, if they want to eat they go to another box, if they want clothes to hide their nakedness they go to another box and move more paper around, whatever they want they go to a box for it, if they want more paper to move around there are great big boxes holding thick-walled metal boxes full of more paper, it's all a great big box, and at the end of the day, they go back to their own little box, exhausted both physically and emotionally, and if they want to remember the earth at all, they grow little square patches of grass in boxes in the ground, it's all boxes and they cant get out, they dont want to get out—those boxes are heated against the cold of the night and cooled against the heat of the day and the monkeys in them dont even know there are seasons anymore, their entire lives are boxed up so nice and neat

and the worst part of it, the worst boxes are the

ones inside their heads—it's a fucking joke

here's the joke—a guy walks into a bar, big grin on his face, he throws some money on the bar, he says, give me a shot of your best whiskey, I'm celebrating—the bartender pours him a shot, the guy puts it back in one gulp, says, gimme another, the bartender pours it, the guy puts it back the same way, the bartender is impressed, he says, what are you celebrating?—the guy says, I just had my first blow job, the bartender says congratulations, that deserves one on the house, and pours him another, the guy knocks it back—he says, keep pouring till I get the taste out of my mouth

very funny, right—but that's one of the boxes, it's two or three of the boxes, all in one place, and you dont even recognize it until you're outside of those boxes—first of all, it assumes that semen has a bad taste, it doesnt, it can be sweet or starchy, but it's not a big yick like the joke implies—the joke also assumes that being a cocksucker is something to be ashamed of, getting a blow job is a good thing, but giving it is bad—except how many of those men want their wives to give them head, isn't that a little hypocritical, disrespectful, misogynistic, why do you want your wife to be a cocksucker if it's a bad thing, and if it's really a good thing to make a man happy, then why dont you praise it—

here—here's the way to tell that joke—an excited teenager runs into the house and says to his dad, I just got my first blow job today, and the dad says, good for you son, I'm proud of you, and the son says, yeah—and it tasted great—except that's not a joke anymore, just a big smile of memory—because we've been there, most of us, and we know it's great, just as good to give as to receive

and that's the point, that's the kind of box they live in, and not the only one, their heads are full of little boxes that keep them ashamed of themselves, too ashamed to suck at the big cock of life, or the big tit, whatever is in front of them, they dont know how to live inside their own bodies, and just enjoy being a naked ape—they're box-monkeys

it's a trap and a tragedy, and the only relief they get is a little booze and maybe a joint and an occasional fuck, and they think that's living, hell if it is, it's a living hell—but you guys, here—you're the only monkeys who have a chance to see that

you're out here, in the clean desert air, you're outside the box, you can see things they cant—some of you, you think they locked you out—

Red held my hand a little tighter when Sterge said that, just enough that I knew that arrow had struck home

—you think they locked you out, no they didnt, they locked themselves in, you should be grateful for the adventure they gave you, you get to be out here under the stars, look at them, ohgod, just look at that glory, yeah, look—that's what you never get to see cowering in a box—oh man, you guys are so

we were so whatever, there wasnt a word for it yet

at the end of the evening, Sterge reached out for Shine's hand, and Shine—what was he thinking?—Shine took the invitation, he took Sterge's hand and they went off into the dark together

I dont know how the others felt, I know I felt inspired and violated, both at the same time

yeah, Shine was only human, just like the rest of us, why shouldnt he get to fuck just like the rest of us—except, why Sterge, this glittery drop-in who hadnt yet lifted anything heavier than a fork

Red held me at night, we talked about trust

"I dont know what trust is," I said, "but if I knew what it was, and if I knew how to do it, I would trust you." I kissed him gently, the way men are supposed to kiss

"I know," he said. "It's a long journey back. But

just being able to say it—that's trust."

"I want to trust you," I said. "I want to trust Shine. I want to trust everyone here."

"One day, you will—no, one day you'll realize you've been trusting us for a long time and didn't know it."

I didnt have an answer for that, nothing I could say aloud—instead, I asked, "Why did Shine let that guy talk all night? It's our circle, not his."

"Shine knows him. From before. I think he's one of the guys he used to sleep with back in school, where they planned the 'mune, everything—the whole idea of reinvention."

"Oh," I said. "So why didnt he come out here with Shine to help start it—?"

"I dunno. I think maybe he had to finish a bunch of other stuff first—some kind of research or training or something—but Shine obviously, y'know—Shine still thinks he's part of it—"

I pulled him closer.

"You okay?" he asked.

"Yeah," I said. "I'm just—I dunno—I wasnt ready for any of that—"

"It kinda made sense, I think."

"Yeah, but so what? I mean, what do we do with it? We get to pretend we're better than the townies—? Because they're monkeys in boxes and we're not? Is that gonna get the latrine dug?"

Red snuggled into my embrace—"Sometimes you're too practical, Chase. It's one of the things I like about you."

"Yeah. I learned the hard way. Having a warm place to shit is a lot more practical than looking at stars—"

"But you like it when we walk out to look at the stars—"

"Sure I do, but I like having a warm place to shit too. So call me a monkey in a box. I also like booze and joints and an occasional fuck. Dont you?"

Red didnt answer—not with words anyway, it was a long pleasant night and I forgot about Sterge and Shine real quick—Red was lean and sinewy and enthusiastic, rocking against me in delicious rhythm until we both came at the same time and collapsed gasping into each other's breathless kiss

if I ever fall in love, I want it to be like this

in the morning, I went out and finished digging the new latrine—you do that not just for yourself, but for everyone else who needs to shit

Sterge stayed for a while, not just the weekend, longer than that—it was his vacation from the monkey boxes, he had to go back and fight the monkey battles—like it or not, the 'mune needed a monkey lawyer and a monkey banker and a monkey liaison, that's how Sterge described it, and the rest of us laughed appreciatively, but if there was an edge to it too, was I the only who felt cut—

another night, he talked about monkeys again—his metaphor, okay—we were the new monkeys, he said, knowledge and technology were a liberating curse—a curse because we didnt know how to be the new monkeys yet, but a chance at liberation if we used the tech to escape the boxes we'd been building for a thousand, two thousand, ten thousand years

in the world we'd inherited, sex was about everything except sex, it was about money and marriage and property and children—but what if we lived in a world without money or property, would we still need marriage to define our relationships, think about it—men without women, we're a different species, shouldn't we have a culture of our own? The 'mune—this is the place where we invent it

"I'll tell you something else," Shine said. "I'm not supposed to. I signed a confidentiality agreement, but—that's box-monkey thinking. What I found out needs to be shared, needs to be known—" and with those words, he had us—"there's this place, I won't say where, it's back there—" he pointed east, as if that explained everything

"There're these people, doctors, a man and a woman, I'm not gonna mention their names, I'm not even supposed to say I was one of their study subjects, even after they publish, because they dont want us giving interviews, but I gotta share this with you, because they're doing something nobody's ever done before—they wire people up with electrodes, and they have them jack off, and they have them fuck each other—they're trying to find out what happens to the human body when you're fucking, they're studying the science of sex, this is the first time in history anybody's ever done something like this

"I heard they were looking for people, so I volunteered—there were forms to fill out, a lot of questions to answer, interviews, everything you can imagine, a complete medical exam, and finally they asked me if I liked boys or girls better, they said they were specifically looking for ho-mo-sex-uals—now I never used that word, never called myself a homosexual, never even thought of myself as homosexual, but the way they said it, I started getting turned on, a lot, yeah—homosexual, that sounds like fun—so I told them, yeah I'd rather do it with a guy and they said, okay, like it was perfectly normal to say that—well, it is, but most people dont know that—

"Anyway, a few days later, they called me in, there's another guy my age, maybe a little older, but not bad-looking—I wouldn't push him out of bed for eating crackers—and they wire us up and tell us to go to it, I stop and ask, "is there anything particular you want us to do?" and they say, no—just do it—okay, they're behind this glass window, watching, we get on the bed and we bump together a while, and then we suck each other for a while, all the stuff you do before the main event, and the main event was pretty good too—

"They called me back a lot, I did it with the same guy again, then I did it with other guys too—I did it with a lot of different guys, some more than once, and we did it a lot of different ways, I got laid more times, I had more sex in just those few months than in all the years since I first shoved my hand into my diaper to play with myself

"I think they liked me, I'm pretty sure they liked me, after a while they treated me like I was one of their favorite porn stars, and one day, one of the assistants, a guy, maybe he was a ho-mo-sex-ual too, I didn't ask, but if he'd ever wired himself up and climbed onto the bed, I'd have done him—enthusiastically—I mean, I think he liked me as much as I would have liked to like him—

"Anyway, we were in the cafeteria, the institute had a little coffee shop attached, and he sits down opposite me and we talk, he thanks me for being such a good subject, I tell him I enjoy the work, we both laugh, except by now, by this stage of the research, we've exhausted all the embarrassment and all the jokes, and we just hop on the bed and get to it—so I ask him, are they getting good results?

"His eyes go wide with delight, he gets a big grin on his face, he leans forward like he's going to share the most amazing secret—'I shouldn't be telling you this,' he says, 'but I think you already know it—' and I say, 'What—that homos have better sex?' and his expression goes all surprised, 'Who told you—?'

"I tell him, nobody, it just seems obvious, to me anyway, especially after all the sex I've been having, courtesy of the institute—because there's so many great things two guys can do with each other, and not just the obvious things either—he stops me in time, I'm already getting a boner, just talking about it, another ten seconds I'd have asked if we should go to his place or mine—but never mind, he says he was in a meeting where they were collating results—

"He tells me that the purpose of the study wasn't homosexuality, but they wanted to study male sexual rhythms and responses all on their own, without any distortions that might come from a woman's biological rhythms and such, the only way to do that was have two men fuck—and the same for women, how do you study female sexual responses free of any effects of having a man involved, you get two women to do it, so that worked out pretty good, they got to study the male sexual responses and the female, each isolated from the other, pretty smart, eh?

"Except—and this was the part he told me—they were collating all the separate results, looking for trends, and they kept bumping into this one that puzzled them at first, then surprised them, then when—when they took the time to think about it—they realized it was kinda inevitable. A guy knows his own body, the most sensitive places, that little place on the front of the dick, just under the helmet, the slickness of the sides, all the way down to the base of the shaft where that extra little squeeze goes joyously screaming all the way up to a G chord above high C—everything, that's what all those years of jacking off are for—it's practice, and once you know what it feels like when you do this or when you do that, you know what to do, and it only makes sense that the other guy is going to know the same things, he's been practicing too—you touch him in the places you like, the way you like, you do to him what you want him to do to you, he's doing the same, it works pretty good, most of the time, I mean, if you're versatile that way—and I guess the same is true with women—

"So that's what they found, two guys are more sensitive to each other's physical needs, two women too—homosex is more tender, more sensitive, more affectionate, call it what you will—it's better. It's enough to make you feel sorry for all the grims—that's what I call them, if we're gay, then they're grims—

"The thing is, they haven't said it yet, but it's true—what we have is special, it's good, it's great, it's better—and that should tell you something about the universe's plan for us, because think about it—" Sterge was excited now, his eyes blazing with the fires of his sexual aspirations, "—think about what this means as an evolutionary mechanism, we're supposed to be this way, it's no accident, there's a reason and a purpose why our sexual connections are better, our intimacies—

"We're the next small step in human evolution! Part of it anyway!"

Sterge took a breath. "I dont think they'll ever publish that part of the study—that our sex is better. I think it made them uncomfortable, I think they found it too disturbing, but we know it now, and it's something we need to know—because now we dont have to listen to what the grims are saying about us. This isn't just validation—it's affirmation. It's liberation!"

and from there to the next step was such a small step, it didnt need any logic, it was just the next place on the path—where he wanted to go anyway—and the other guys, all caught up in the excitement, they ran right after

and—

okay, yeah, in the fevered heat of the fire pit, under the cold bright stars, naked to the Arizona night, stoned on our own delusions—yeah, we were ready to dance and shout, banging rocks together over our heads, painting ourselves with stripes of red and black—we're the new monkeys, the naked monkeys, the queer monkeys, tearing it all down, all those opinions and beliefs that were poured into our heads, abandoning the past, shouting defiance to the sky, creating chaos in the night to challenge the obsolete gods and monsters of the past, shredding the ideas of yesterday—

we're the new humanity, naked monkeys, drunk and stoned and horny, arrogantly celebrating our superior masculinity, waving our dicks at each other, our skyward-pointing erections, each a personal mandate—if we had each other, we were in a better place than all those people who'd denied us our identities—we didnt need women, therefore we didnt need to have our sexuality, our relationships, our physical connections defined by box-monkeys and women and all the grims with all their grim fairy tales about how we were sinners and deviates, perverts and degenerates, because now we had proof that we weren't, we had scientific evidence—thank you, Sterge—that who we are and what we have isn't just something special, it's something superior, so from there it's just one small step to say, it's our job here to define and invent and create a true homosexual identity—

even if it was bullshit, it was beautiful bullshit and I wanted to believe in something better than just being another horny oxygen-sucker, and that night, something happened, maybe it was just really really good dope, but something happened, and we *pinged* and for a moment, just a moment, I was outside everything, outside my own body, outside of the world, and at the same time, I was inside, inside all of us, I could feel what everyone else was feeling, I *knew* it all—and I knew they did too—and then it was over and it was morning and I swear to you, this is true, I woke up laughing, literally laughing, at I dont know what, and I sat up, and I saw that the others were up too, we were all blinking in the dawn, the sun hadnt come up yet, but there were two kinds of darkness at the horizon, above and below, and pretty soon the above darkness started shading from black to dark gray, and from there to light gray to white to pink to yellow to blue, crisp beautiful blue, so deep and aching you couldnt see the end of it, and we all just sat there, waiting in silence, and finally we looked at each other and started laughing again, because we knew that we were indelibly linked somehow—we were *pinged*

and no, we didnt talk about it, we couldnt, there arent any words in the English language, although there are some people who've tried, mostly people fumbling around for the future, they talk about hiveminds and massminds and a collective consciousness, more than human, and shit like that, but none of those words come anywhere near what happened, because what happened didnt happen in language, it happened in reality—and talking about it, even this conversation, right here, right now, with you, just collapses it into a bunch of symbols, words, try to type it up and it turns into crawly little insect marks on a page—but that's where the *pings* came from—and in the morning, Sterge was gone, and as much as we wanted, as much as we tried, we werent able to *ping* again, and after a while, knowing what was possible and knowing we couldnt get back there, something changed

evaporated

I mean, we tried, oh god, we tried. We got so stoned so many times, each time trying to find that right combination—but it didnt work, couldnt work, because we were trying—it only happens when you're not trying to make it happen, so it's fucking impossible—and yet, the thing is, knowing that it's possible, that's the joke, knowing that it's possible makes it inevitable, you just cant want it, it has to happen by itself—

so most of us, we settled for fucking instead, which was okay, really—but it was nothing near what we really wanted

in that single evening of orgiastic abandon, Sterge had turned us inside out, he took us to the top of a mountain

and then let us tumble down the slope afterward

sometimes it gets all confused in my head, maybe Sterge was right, for just that little moment, that six-inch moment of delight, I wanted him to be right, but what if he wasn't—what if he was just another self-deluded, twenty-something, self-inflated ideologue, spurting and spouting his frenzied sex-addled ideas—all that stuff that sounds great in the middle of the night, when you're drunk and stoned and horny, but evaporate like dew in the crisp clear dawn when pink sunlight stretches sideways across the Arizona desert and you still have to get up and hoe the weeds out of the potatoes and your body is saying, fuck it's too cold to let go of Red, and get out from under this blanket, too cold even to pee—but I gotta pee and I gotta get up because I gotta get up, fuck it anway

and standing there, my dick in my hand, the hot piss splattering into the dry ground, all that nighttime ache draining out of me, leaving the resonating echo of itself as a whole other kind of ache, the bright wind making me wake up despite myself, all I could think was 'what the fuck was that all about?' and the darker thought that I didnt know, hadnt had the same experience, but maybe the human heart doesnt work the way Sterge said—it sounded good, yeah—but maybe evolution didnt work like that, maybe evolution made us another way instead, that men are designed to complement women somehow, I dunno—I'm not an expert on women, never will be, too much time in bed with men and not enough time any other way

but if anyone else was frowning in puzzlement, I didnt see it—for a while I thought I was being left behind, it was my fault that I couldnt keep up they were so sure of themselves

and I was fulminating in doubt, a rising conversation of confusion

what if Sterge was right? I kinda wanted him to be right, but I kinda didnt want that either

because then I'd have to stop being who I was and start being someone I wasnt, someone I didnt know how to be

oh fuck

because the more I thought about it, the more I thought that maybe this time I really should leave, because if I couldnt keep up, I was holding them back

but I remembered what happened the last time I'd ridden off, and how I'd come back and Red had been waiting for me, and—I didnt want to leave Red, I liked him in the daytime, I liked him at night, I liked the way he felt in my arms, I wasnt ready to give that up, the way he would curl up in my arms and the affectionate way he would call me daddy, even though I was only seven years older than him, but I was more daddy than his real parent had been, because I wasnt the one who pushed him out into the night, unloved—so we'd walk out into the desert under the glow of the Milky Way—

and in those moments, I knew

Red was the 'mune, the son, and the stars—he was the bright side of the 'mune

he was all those silly beautiful clichés rolled into one—only made flesh-and-blood real, a hard body, a hard cock, all the hardness that pushed back against me, harder than hard, everything I needed, wanted, and held onto so desperately every night

jeez, I was sick with man-madness, wrapped up and enraptured, infatuated with the flood of endorphins, still learning how to be together comfortably, constantly needing the whispered reassurances that everything was going to be all right—because inside, I'd never known that feeling for myself that anything was going to be all right

and I was right, I'm always right, I hate being right, I want to be wrong about this shit, just once—but it never happens that way, because while I clung so tightly to Red

the next time Sterge came back, a few weeks later, everything was different—because we had the memory now, and the memory changed us, we wanted to stay in that delicious soaring moment of last week, we were stuck in the past and all the repetitions of 'be here now, let's live in the present' were belied by the word 'again'—and now the 'mune was churning with some kind of hunger

addiction is the memory of pleasure—that's where it starts, but it sucks you in like the proverbial two-dollar whore—the guys said they wanted to *ping* again—but it was the 'again' that gave them away, it wasnt about connecting anymore, that was a lie, an excuse, a story, the justification for what they did instead—that was the 'mune pretending they hadnt turned into a pack of sex junkies looking hungrily for six inches more of pink needle

it was the perfect setup for Sterge, he started fucking his way through the 'mune like—I dunno—like a cock-machine skewering his conquests *en brochette*, one at a time, then all at once, first Shine of course, then Van, then Caleb, then all four of them at once, then he started working on Brownie and Bear, and everyone so hungry to *ping* they waggled their tight little asses like Catholic schoolgirls desperate to be mounted while their hormones were surging—Shine was lost to us, he went all glassy eyed, following Sterge like a shadow, nodding in raptured acquiescence

it was orgy-time, that's what Sterge brought to the 'mune—and the thing about orgies, I only learned this later, is that they're disrespectful, they're not about people, they're about bodies, they're about sensation, they're about rolling around in a frenzy of 'I'll have some of this and I'll have some of that'—but never is there the deeper appreciation that comes with 'I want to connect, as deep as I can, with this one single entity opposite me, I want to know who you are to the depth of your soul and let you grab onto as much of mine as you can bear to hold—'

yeah, that's the point

I dont mind being a naked monkey, after all this time I'm getting pretty good at it—I mind being a stupid naked monkey

when the fucking started, when it turned into orgies, I took Red by the hand and walked him into the dark beneath the stars, "I'd rather be with you," I told him, and I thought that was enough

Red squeezed my hand, and I thought he was agreeing with me, but then he said, "This is the 'mune, we dont own each other."

"No, we dont," I agreed, because even though I didnt agree, I wouldnt speak my disagreement—"I'm just saying I'd rather be with you," hoping for the same words from him

instead, he just squeezed my hand

and if I'd been smart enough to understand language of hand-holding, I would have turned around and gotten on my hog and left before the rest of the sky fell in

two afternoons later, I found Red in bed with Sterge—I shouldnt have been surprised, Sterge was working his way across the 'mune, like a warrior on a mission, in this case the mission to fuck everyone and fuck up everything

I backed out of the teepee, embarrassed, maybe I should have been angry, but anger would have been even more embarrassing, we were supposed to be enlightened naked monkeys

later Red came to me while I was polishing the bike, that should have been a signal to him right there, but he came to me anyway and asked, "are we good" and when I didnt answer, he asked, "why are you upset?" and I said, "what do you think?" and he said, "but it's only sex, it's not like it means anything," and that was the worst thing he could have said to me, I didnt look up, I tightened my face and somehow got the words out, "it means something to me," and he said, "that's not very enlightened," and that's when I turned to him and let him have it, the whole fucking clip, rapid fire, I said, "yeah, I know—but I grew up in a place where sex didnt mean anything and I sold myself on Santa Monica Boulevard because sex didnt mean anything and I was all over Nam where sex didnt mean anything and you know what, Red—that's bullshit, just fucking bullshit, all of it—because if sex doesnt mean anything then nothing means anything, none of this, none of us—I aint Sterge and I aint Shine and I didnt go to no expensive fancy university to learn multi-syllable justifications like 'transformation' and 'reinvention'—all I know is that after all I been through, all I got is me, that's it—everything, the only thing, just me—that's all I got to give anyone, so if I give me to someone, I want them to give themselves back, the same hundred and ten percent, and if that's selfish, then yeah, I'm a selfish fucking monkey—and if I'm a selfish fucking monkey then I'm not ready to be part of this 'mune or any other 'mune—not if it means that fucking doesnt mean anything, because I been there and back—it's a long way back, I learned that the hard way, so you choose—either fucking means something to you or it doesnt, and if it doesnt then you can kiss me goodbye, starting right here on my big fat ass 'cause I'm not putting up with anyone's bullshit just because he calls it 'enlightenment'—"

maybe I should have stopped somewhere in the middle of that, maybe I shouldnt have said any of it,

Red looked like I'd smacked him in the face, I could almost see the splotch of the handprint reddening, he said, "I'm sorry, I thought you were someone else," and he turned and ran away

yeah, well—maybe I'd thought I was someone else too, but now I knew I wasnt

well, fuck

I turned back to the bike and just stared at my reflection, squeezed sideways in the shining chrome, I couldnt see anything but my own rage, and then, just when I figured I couldnt make things any worse, Sterge wandered over, maybe Red had said something to him and maybe he thought he was going to fix the situation, like he was so enlightened he could make anybody think anything, or maybe it was just that I was the only one left he hadnt fucked yet—whatever, he started off by saying, "nice bike," and I just grunted and kept cleaning, even though I'd already cleaned that part a dozen times, but if I didn't keep cleaning the bike, the desert was going to sandpaper it away, Sterge hunkered down next to me, he was wearing one of those gauzy white shirts they make somewhere in India and a pair of Shine's cutoffs, he smelled of incense and oils and he'd braided his hair with little beads twisted into the strands, his way of dressing the part I guess

he said, "I dont get you, Chase"—I just shrugged in response, I didnt care if he got me or not, so fucking what, he'd helped himself to something that he shouldnt have, he shoulda respected what was there—but it wasnt just his fault, Red shoulda known better too, but right then I was mostly mad at Sterge, he wasnt us, no matter how hard he pretended to be, and he'd used us, one at a time, and the hard ugly truth was that we werent *us* at all, at least not anymore, because Sterge had turned us into something else, and the more he talked, the more I understood why I was polishing the bike

"I get it," he said, "I get why you're upset, guy, it's a natural reaction, but it's a box-monkey reaction—it's you assuming ownership where there is none, you cant own another person, man, that's slavery—that's why we're all out here, to be free—"

I was still angry, it didnt show, because I'd calmed down enough by then to be in that much more dangerous place—that place where I can choose to be dangerous—Sterge didnt know me well enough to know the danger signs, he really didnt know half as much as he pretended

I finally said to him, "You and I, we have different definitions of freedom—or maybe we're just looking for different things, I dunno what freedom is, the best I can say is that it's all about being able to choose, if you have choices, you're free, and if you dont then you aint—

he frowned, that was his way of showing you he was listening, he wore his listening frown, I stared hard into his face, "You had a choice, you coulda done this, you coulda done that—you chose the one instead of the other—okay, that's what you chose, but whenever you choose something, guy, you also choose the consequences—" he started to protest, but I held up a hand, "no, it's my turn to talk—I heard you, everything you said, you talk good, better'n me, that's fine, but here's what I do know—I know I cant tell you what to do or what not to do, 'cause you're gonna do whatever it is you're gonna do, no matter what anyone says, that's just you—you have all your choices, and you been choosing us like things on a menu, but that doesnt mean I gotta like it, and I dont, because I dont think that's what we're supposed to be doing here, and yeah—maybe I'm wrong about that too—maybe you're right about everything, it sure sounds good, hell, it sounds great, and maybe some people will be convinced, maybe some people will go along with you, and that's their choice too—but I aint some people—"

"No, you're not," he said, "you're someone special—" he put his hand on my shoulder, I shook it off—"dont be that way, I'm tryin' to connect with you," and that's when I stood up and he stood up too and for a moment, I just glared at him, "Listen up, man—you need to get this and you need to get it good, I dont wanna connect with you or anyone else here in this 'mune, you fucked it up—I thought it was what I wanted, but maybe it wasnt what I thought it was, because when you showed up, you turned it into what you wanted—and what you want, well, it's pretty fucked up, at least that's how it looks to me—because I thought Red and I had something good, or maybe we were on the way there, but it was something and now it's nothing, because you think your dick is so important that other people's feelings dont matter, and as long as I'm talking, I might as well say the rest of it, I think you're a phony, and all that charm and bullshit still doesnt hide what a selfish fuck you are—"

"I see there's no chance of a dialog here," he said, and I said, "yeah, you blew that away when you blew my boyfriend—"

"He was never your boyfriend—"

"Yeah, and thanks for that too—I'm glad I found that out before I wasted any more time there—"

twenty minutes later, I was gone, hurtling down the broken black road to anywhere

fuck and fuck and fuck

and behind me, at the circle, I knew what they were saying, because by now I knew them well enough to know that brand of bullshit, "well, we loved Chase, we'll always love him, but he has his own stuff to deal with now, so let's send good vibes his way, and blah blah blah—all that crap they say to excuse their own responsibility in the matter, you think I'm fooled, fuck no and maybe yeah, down the road a bit, I'm gassing up the hog with the last of my paper, I'm at one of those stations so old, the cockroaches are in wheelchairs, and I dont get on the bike, I just walk off to a bench nearby, carved out of a petrified log sliced lengthwise and polished to a shine, how did they do that anyway if this thing is petrified, it doesnt matter, and I sit down and light a joint, not caring who knows, and I'm thinking, fuck, what if they're right, what if I really am a selfish asshole, trying to own Red, what if Sterge is right about box-monkeys and naked monkeys and sex being a way for men to

see, that was the conversation that I couldnt shake—Sterge said that when two men meet and look at each other, they're sizing each other up, can I take him, which one of us is the alpha here—that's what box-monkeys do

but when two queers meet, they dont do that—well, yes they do, but differently, the question isnt "can I take him?"—it's "will we do it?" or and it doesnt matter if the answer is yes or no, the unspoken challenge doesnt happen, there's no challenge, there's something else, something that we dont have words for yet, but that's the difference between queers and breeders—breeders look at each other as competition, queers look at each other as possibilities, that's why queers make better friends, maybe—anyway, that's what Sterge said

and if he was right about any of that, then I really did fuck up, because I saw him as a challenge

yeah, I was thinking like a straight guy

I laughed, a short sharp bark

I finally made it, I finally made it

it doesnt matter where I been sticking my dick, I finally fit in with the box-monkeys, somethin' I been tryin' to do since before forever

I found my box

well, fuck me on a pogo stick

what a fucked-up way to be

all that stuff I'd always said—about how people cant ever really be trusted, not them, not me—now I had the last piece of evidence to prove it

yeah, okay, I'll use that ugly four-letter word—*love*—it's a loaded gun, a time bomb, another little hand grenade that goes off in the mud and blows you to hell and gone

if you're not looking for it, you're not going to find it—but even if you are looking for it, that's no guarantee either—and sometimes, if you give up, decide it isnt possible for you, you fall into it anyway, at least until you get kicked out again—because nothing is permanent, life is one long assault and pain is universal and no one here gets out alive

it's an illusion, a delusion, comfortable and delicious and false, just like all the other boxes

and fuck me, anyway—I miss it so much, too much

but I'm still not going back

they might be right about all of that, they might be the best naked monkeys ever, and they might know what enlightenment is from the far side coming back, but what Sterge showed me when he fucked Red in my bed, he showed me—ha ha—the dark side of the 'mune

and I cant bear it, I just cant

so I rattled out of Arizona, it was summer, so I battered up the left coast, heading up to Alaska, where there arent any queers, but there sure are a lot of lonely straight guys who appreciate a helping hand, willing to return the favor, and they dont always care how many legs you got as long as the middle one is working, just dont talk about it and no kissing

gonna take a long time to get over this one, losing your heart is worse than losing your leg, you can get a metal and plastic leg, you can do the physical therapy, and you can cuss and swear and bitch and moan about the pain of rehab, and the nurses and the aides will cheer your every "fuck fuck fuck" as long as you're taking the next step forward

but piss and moan about a broken heart, you're just a whiney little pussy, so shut up already, grit and bear it

okay, you want the punch line, I'll give you several—here's one now—life is one long assault

this is what I know about life—there aint anything else, it's just a little flicker of awareness in the middle of darkness, it isnt heaven, it isnt hell, it's just right here, right now

it's brutal, it's chaotic, it's a sprawling mess that makes no sense, it's a haphazard heap of garbage that you dig through, desperately, frantically, looking for the sparkly parts

it's whatever we make it, and most of the time we dont make it—we just attach a lot of shoulda-coulda-woulda to the stories we tell and pretend we're being courageous when we get back up to receive the next pie in the face—if it knocks you down, it was well delivered, you're on your back tasting the rancid custard of circumstances—if you can get back up, you can pretend to be enlightened and call it a learning experience, but that doesnt make it hurt any less

and you keep getting these pies, these cream-of-pickle confections, until the last one, the big one that goes off like a fumbled grenade, the one that finally knocks you flat on your face, splatting into the ditch of muddy oblivion

at best, it's a mad fucking caucus race, at worst it's a waiting game—either way the end is the same, rigor mortis

sometimes I wonder, whatever happened to the 'mune—did it work out for them, or did it evaporate like all the other hippie experiments of the time—I never really found out

a decade later, coasting across the southwest again, I found myself on that same road, accidental or on purpose, sometimes my head plays tricks— or maybe I was finally over it and curious to see if anything was left, or anyone, but at the end of that bumpy dirt road, there was nothing, just a few scars on the land where a few things had been, but the desert winds had finally scraped most of it away, there were some nice sunflowers growing where the compost pit had been, that made me smile, but other than that

there was nothing else here, nothing to indicate what had happened to the 'mune or where anyone had gone, I didnt even know their last names, so even if I wanted to go searching for them, which I didnt, I wouldnt know how or where or what I was searching for, but see—that's the thing, despite the crap that went down, my crap, theirs, anyone's, it didnt matter anymore, there had been something there, even if only for a moment—maybe not a realized dream, but a possibility of a dream

and yeah, who wouldnt want that, because even a possibility is a helluva lot more than nothing

I got nothing

now get the fuck outa here and let me die

—nothing happens—

sixteen o'clock in the morning

sixteen o'clock and I didn't die

the van was gone, totaled in the crash

the leg too—that was totaled too

so when the nurse wheeled me to the front door of the hospital, I literally (in the literal meaning of the word literally) did not have a leg to stand on, I had a crutch to lean on, and they wanted that back, or $145, which they were going to add to my bill—yeah, come after me for that, after I win the lotto

wheeled to the front door and dumped on the sidewalk, bye now, have a nice day

didnt know which way to turn

and there's Michael, big stupid Michael, big stupid grin on his big stupid face

"What the fuck are you doing here?"

"Thought you might need a ride." He pats the fender of his blue Honda.

"To where?"

"Anywhere you want."

"I got nothing. Just these clothes they found for me. Where am I going to go?"

"Can't stay here—"

"Not at these prices—"

I get in the car, he gets in the other side, we pull

away from the curb. "Why are you doing this? Why do you keep coming back?"

"Because," he says. "Everything you said. I listened. I heard you."

"Big fucking whoop. So what—"

"So what?" His voice rises. He says, "Sometimes, Chase, you are so fucking blind and stupid, you gotta have your nose rubbed in it. *It happened!* You got out there and drove through life at a hundred and sixty miles an hour. Did you ever stop to look at where you were? Where you'd been? Where you were going?

"Fuck, man! The *pings!* You found it, maybe only a little piece of it, and maybe not for very long, and even if it was only for a few weeks or a few months, you had it, man—and now you know something most of the rest of us box-monkeys have never known. Might never know at all. What you had, you had the real, not the pretend. You. Had. It. And fuck you—you brought some of it back out with you, whatever it is—and I want it too. Whatever it is."

I shut up. I have nothing to say.

We drive in silence. While the words sink in. All the way down.

Finally. "So...where are we going?"

Michael smiles. "I thought we'd go out to the desert. And look at the stars. And after that...who the hell knows, but we'll figure it out."

—whatever happens—

Author's Afterword

This is not a memoir. It is not an autobiography. It is not a confession.

Some of the locations portrayed in this book are based on places that once existed.

Some of the situations portrayed in this book are based on actual incidents.

Some of the minor characters portrayed in this book are very loosely based on actual people I have met.

But please do not assume that I am revealing any deep dark secrets about my own fevered history.

I am not.

I am saving those for another book.

Thank you.

— David Gerrold

About the Author

David Gerrold has been writing professionally for half a century. He created the tribbles for *Star Trek* and the Sleestaks for *Land Of The Lost*. His most famous novel is *The Man Who Folded Himself*. His semi-autobiographical tale of his son's adoption, "The Martian Child" won both the Hugo and the Nebula awards, and was the basis for the 2007 movie starring John Cusack and Amanda Peet.

You can find more about him at http://www.gerrold.com.

CPSIA information can be obtained
at www.ICGtesting.com
Printed in the USA
LVOW04*0010110816
499882LV00007B/10/P

2 370000 255747